REDEEMING

Virtually Mine

a love story

SUSAN ROHRER

Infinite Arts Media

VIRTUALLY MINE: a love story
(Redeeming Romance Series)
Written by Susan Rohrer
Adapted from Susan Rohrer's original screenplay

Kindly direct professional inquiries about this novel or screenplay to:
InfiniteArtsMgmt@gmail.com

Readers may contact author at:
shelfari.com/susanrohrer

ISBN 13: 978-1482378948
ISBN 10: 1482378949

Published in the United States of America

Second Edition 2016

To every reader
who looks beyond the eye-candy coating
to the heart that beats underneath

contents

one

Kate Valentine's heart skipped a beat. She'd told herself that the troupe of thespians had left, that she'd been alone, retrieving plastic prop apples on the darkened stage, but no. There he was, lingering.

She glanced up with a sweet smile, in a futile attempt at nonchalance. As a small town import to the big city, Kate could pull it off with other guys. She could overcome her shy nature. But in this surreal context, even a glimpse of this particular actor's rakishly handsome face rocked her world, a great deal more than she dared to admit.

Kate reminded herself that there were protocols to observe. In the politics of the theater, he was light years out of her league. He was Dustin Hunt. He'd been cast as the leading man, and her role was only that of the lowly prop girl, and a first-timer at that.

It's not that Kate hadn't given vent to fantasy. She'd played this scene out in her mind more times than she could count, in vivid and varied detail. She'd rehearsed what she'd do, exactly how she'd respond in an imagination rife with possibilities. But this was no dream, no flight of fancy. This scene that had seemed utter whimsy had now burst into wide-awake life.

She was in the moment, alone with him.

Jauntily, Dustin moved in from the wings.

Kate stashed another apple into the crook of her arm. "Oh, hi. I'd really... I thought I was alone."

"Would you rather be?"

This guy had a way of getting under her skin and tickling every cell inside of her. From the mischievous sparkle in his eyes, she could tell it was his objective to achieve precisely that. She resolved to mask the fact that he was succeeding. "No. I just thought I was. Alone."

"Because I can go," he offered, an assured expression betraying his confidence that she wanted him there.

"It's okay. Really. I'm practically—"

Kate wasn't normally a clumsy person. But this situation wasn't normal. Being on that stage with Dustin knocked the balance she clung to completely off center. *Oh no*, she worried. She could feel her grip loosening, but somehow she couldn't stop it. Faux apples avalanched out of her grasp.

They bounced. They clunked. They rolled.

Instantly, Kate felt her face redden. Rampant blotching around her throat would come next. It was one of those ways she was wired that was completely beyond her control. She could only drop to her knees awkwardly and gather the fugitive fruit.

She stopped, suddenly sensing his nearness. Even before she braved to tip her eyes up, she could tell that he was there. Right there. *Go with this,* she coaxed herself.

Slowly, Kate lifted her head. She startled to find herself nose to nose with him. *What exactly is his intent?* She couldn't help but wonder. Her breath short, she bravely held her ground. She would not let the moment escape her. She would not back down.

"Are you going to help me?" she managed.

"Do you want me to?"

"I'm not sure," she whispered, dazed by his proximity. There he was, his impossibly adorable face mere inches away, those dancing green eyes looking deep into hers. Warm breath wafted toward her. He smelled of peanut butter, she realized. She liked peanut butter.

Dustin closed his eyes and slowly leaned toward her. She couldn't believe it was happening, but then again, it was. Her lids fluttered to a close, as they moved together for a sweetly uncertain, tender kiss.

Suddenly interrupting, scene study teacher Antonio Spirelis rose to address a sizable class of on-looking thespians. He clapped his hands sharply, bringing the group back to reality. "Okay, that's the scene. Disengage, people."

On stage, acting students Kate and Dustin obediently broke character. They curtailed their scripted smooch. Kate gave Dustin's hand a fond squeeze. The acted kiss had come naturally, since Dustin was her real-life beau. She'd been smitten with him since they'd first met, but something in the exhilaration of playing this scene in class together had been like falling for him all over again.

Antonio turned to his class. "Let's dissect." As Kate and Dustin sat cross-legged on the stage, Antonio swaggered before the class. "All right—Dustin, Kate. What is the event of the scene?"

Dustin turned blankly to Kate. Hoping to help, Kate hazarded a guess. "The kiss?"

"That's there in the text," Antonio reminded. "What subtextural event brings about the kiss?"

Smolderingly savvy, twenty-five year-old Wissy Frank piped up. "Change of relationship."

Antonio nodded. "Very good, Ms. Frank. Why did it change? Dustin?"

"Because she's hot," Dustin observed, clearly enjoying the laughs he elicited from his peers.

Antonio raised his hand, quieting the class. "Was she hot before? Fifteen minutes ago? Why now? Kate?"

Kate glanced at Dustin, but he just shrugged, stumped. Engagingly bright, but fairly new to the acting process, answers sometimes evaded Kate. Charmingly, she grimaced. "Because, well, the writer wrote it that way and—"

"And left you to discover what's underneath," Antonio finished. "What made this particular encounter different than any prior one? Not the words. What goes on inside of us, and then manifests itself in radically altered behavior? What quietly happens when one person looks at another, even a complete stranger, and the way they relate to one another is forever changed?"

The Third Street Promenade was rife with activity as Antonio's acting class dispersed. Kate stepped aside with her cell phone as shoppers mingled past street performers, vying for a break in the business, or at least tips in their cups.

Kate scooted by a talent scout with a clipboard.

"Excuse me", the scout said. "I'm casting for a reality dating show."

Kate responded cheerily. "Thanks, but I'm in a relationship."

Wasting no time, the scout turned to another prospect. "Hey...looking for love?"

"Yeah, who isn't?" the prospect groused.

Kate sighed gratefully. It felt good to be off the dating market. She punched in her parents' speed-dial and plugged her free ear. Kate enjoyed the fact that she could be in the middle of a California crowd, but at the very same time, she could be across the country in her mother's kitchen, near the foot of Afton Mountain, in sleepy little Crozet, Virginia. She could see the real apples her mother was peeling. She could smell the fresh daisies on the counter. She could hear the lilt of her mother's voice and suddenly feel at home.

"So, tell your mom. How's progress."

Kate waved goodbye to Antonio as he threw on his designer sunglasses and turned to leave. "Great, I think. My teacher said he liked my work today."

"I'm talking about with Dustin, Baby. He say the 'M' word yet?"

"Well, the 'L' word usually precedes the 'M' word," Kate whispered, not wanting Dustin to hear.

"He said the 'L' word?"

"Sort of."

"I knew it!" Kate's mom exuded.

"At least I think he's going to." She adored that her mom was just as excited about every detail of her daughter's life as she was about her own.

Kate kept an eye on the object of her affections as he chatted with Wissy nearby. Worry poked its pointy fingers into her heart. "Listen, I've gotta go. Love you, Mom. Hugs to Daddy."

Kate hung up and made her way toward Dustin, just in time to see Wissy hand him her card.

"No, really. It's incredible, isn't it?" Wissy flirted. "But this could be my break, and my break could be your break, making it by extension our break, so think about it."

Dustin smiled broadly. "Definitely."

Wissy glided away as Kate reached Dustin. Kate wrapped her arms around his middle, reclaiming her steady guy.

"I don't care what Antonio says," she assured. "I think you were great."

"I fizzed you, didn't I?"

"Always do." Kate drew Dustin into a real-life kiss. Usually, he did have an effervescent effect. But this time, as Dustin pulled away, Kate distinctly saw him check to see if a departing Wissy was watching. In three months of dating Dustin, it wasn't the first time Kate had seen a pretty girl make a play for him. It was the risk a girl accepted when she dated a cute guy like Dustin, and she reminded herself that she was the one he actually called his girlfriend. "So, you want to start on the next scene tonight?"

Dustin sputtered, this time glancing squarely in Wissy's direction. "Okay, otherwise, I completely would, but see, this is really outstanding. Get this. You know Wissy—just left—well, she gave me her card." Dustin showed off the prize.

Puzzled, Kate examined it. She caught a whiff of night jasmine and noted the local number. Not wanting to betray how vulnerable she felt, Kate played along. Comprehending the feminine mystique wasn't Dustin's strong suit, so she wanted to make sure he really got what Wissy was doing. "And okay, why would I think it's a good thing that an attractive, albeit synthetically enhanced person is throwing herself at my boyfriend?"

"Because she wants to do a scene with me," Dustin dimly enthused.

"Still looking for the outstanding part."

"Big picture, Kate. Wissy isn't really an actress. She's only in class to inform herself. Do you love that? That's what she said. She's informing herself as a casting director to be."

Kate tried her best to stay calm. "Uh-huh."

Dustin's animation grew. "Anyway, Wissy, she completely flipped over my work today, but bottom line—are you ready, Kate? Wissy just got a job as an intern to an assistant to this semi-monstrously important casting director who she's considering pitching me to soon. Only she wants to work with me personally first. You know, she wants to see how I create chemistry with someone other than you. Because after all, we're already bringing in three months of real-life sparks, which tells her nothing about what I can do craft-wise with a more random person like herself."

Kate felt her jaw go slack. Her knees wobbled. The ground seemed to drop out beneath her. *Was that an earthquake?* Living in L.A., she couldn't help wonder, after the way he'd tipped her balance.

"I know! Amazing, right?" Dustin exuded.

She stood there, flabbergasted. He had told her about Wissy's wiles with his own sweet lips, so breathlessly that tiny bubbles of spittle formed in the corners of his mouth, as if there wasn't a thing in the world registering inside his delightfully clueless head.

"Okay, well...I've gotta run to...my apartment and, uh, help my roommate. Yeah, M.J. definitely needs help." Kate knew how ridiculous that sounded when she said it, but it was all she could come up with given the way her mind was reeling.

M.J. Poster keyed in a parking ticket. Were her Meter Maid beat not in sunny Santa Monica, California, the job would have seemed less tolerable. As it was, she'd acclimated to the low-grade contempt most people automatically had for anyone who was in her line of work.

M.J. gazed skyward as a small plane soared above the beach, an advertising banner in tow. *Imagine Yourself in Love*, it read. A web address for a company called *Virtually Mine* was just below. M.J. had no problem imagining what love could be like for her. It was the realities that never quite came to be, given the facts of her work-a-day life.

As many cute guys as were regulars at the bluffside Palisades Park, M.J. knew that citing them with tickets wasn't exactly the optimum kind of how-do-you-do. Besides, she reasoned, her uniform made her look chunky. Not that she actually was chunky, she reassured herself. It was an optical illusion. She was, in fact, just petite—and respectably attractive—both attributes she knew that her boring, standard-issue man-shoes did nothing whatsoever to elevate.

Suddenly, there he was. *Yow*.

M.J. had no idea who he was, but she'd seen him the day before, the same new guy. With that bouncy head of tawny-red hair, he wasn't hard to notice. There he was, jogging on the sandy path again, past many a parked car, in stride with that same golden retriever.

Unexpectedly, he stopped, pulled out a bottle of water, and squirted some into the panting dog's mouth. He hadn't even taken a swig himself first.

Aw, how sweet was that?

Something shifted in M.J. when she saw that rusty-mopped guy and his dog, lapping the water up thirstily. This one was special somehow. He was different and M.J. knew it. Still, there was no way she'd approach him in uniform. In fact, she quickly stuffed the ticket she'd written under a nearby windshield wiper and ducked into her trusty Meter Maid Mobile.

M.J. checked back. No, he hadn't seen her, but she had definitely seen him. And she was truly undone.

Back in the privacy of her kitchen, Kate chopped salad veggies. There was something about making dinner with her salt-of-the-earth roommate that always helped Kate to find her footing. M.J. was still clad in her Meter Maid uniform, except for the much-hated man-shoes that, as usual, she'd kicked off in favor of flip-flops as soon as she'd come into the apartment. Kate peeled and diced with unusual vigor, taking out her frustrations on the produce.

M.J. popped a carrot slice into her mouth. "So, you're telling me Dustin bit on that casting line?"

Kate had to admit it. M.J. had a real talent for slicing straight through the subterfuge, right to the scary, naked truth underneath. "Yeah, he's totally convinced it's this big career move."

"It's a move alright," M.J. intuited.

Kate's face fell. She'd tried so hard to persuade herself that there was no reason to feel threatened. "Maybe it wasn't that kind of move. Maybe she just sees his potential as an actor."

M.J. stripped a stalk of celery insistently. "Kate! Sweetie, you were Phi Beta Carotene, how can you not get this? Some Wissy person—-and by the way, what kind of name is that? So, Wissy thoroughly puts a clamp on your heretofore-exclusive boyfriend right under your cute little nose and, zippidy-do-dah, he's seeing other people."

"He's not seeing other people. It's business." It sounded preposterous to Kate. She knew it, just as soon as she said it. Then again, she wasn't entirely sure. She did her best to cover her insecurity, but M.J. busted her with a look.

"Business."

"Our business is not like yours, M.J."

"No, you're both waiters."

Kate stuffed cucumber peelings down the disposal. "I'm talking about acting. Dustin and me—no, I, Dustin and I—anyway, we have to be able to trust each other. We're both going to be in positions, I mean, please God, hopefully, where we have to at least act like we're attracted to other people. It's part of the job."

"Okay."

"Okay?"

M.J. shrugged. "Okay. Hey, if it doesn't make you crazy that your boyfriend kisses other girls for a living, then I guess you're more secure than I'd ever be. That is, if I actually had a boyfriend in the first place." A girlish smile curled on M.J.'s lips. "Change of subject?"

Kate welcomed the reprieve. "Please."

"So, I saw him again, today."

Still preoccupied, Kate willed herself to take an interest. "Who, him?"

M.J. beamed. "Mr. Nameless But Adorable. Gotta love a guy who's so sweet to his dog."

Unable to let go, Kate blurted. "Wait. Do you really think Dustin wants to see other people? Because isn't that just a euphemism for breaking up? And tell me, how is it that we can possibly be breaking up when my mother is planning our wedding?"

M.J. wryly stepped to the cabinet and pulled out some plates. "Oh, pardon. Did you not detect that the conversation had moved on to matters affecting me?"

Immediately, Kate felt awful. It wasn't at all like her to be so self-absorbed, especially not with M.J. Truth be told, M.J. had been more like a sister than a roommate, ever since Kate had moved west, not knowing a solitary soul. She'd found M.J.'s post on a Roommate Wanted board, something that could be a dicey proposition in L.A. But as different as they were, the two of them had clicked, making a home away from home in the city.

"Sorry. Give me a second, then tell me absolutely everything," Kate repented as she flipped on the garbage disposal.

M.J. heard the sickening ca-chunk as the device quickly jammed. "Houston, we have a problem."

two

Eric Bender scanned his posh surroundings. A sign on the wall of the upscale office space announced that these were the headquarters of a burgeoning business: *Virtually Mine.* Posters of eye-candy models hung on the walls, the faces of this flourishing enterprise. An up-and-coming model himself, Eric relished the opportunity to add his image to theirs.

Eric sized up his new employer as she toured him through the high-tech office pool. Smoothly domineering, Samantha Raznick was a man in a remarkably well-preserved, decidedly female body.

Samantha brushed a manicured hand against Eric's back, guiding him. "It's all about commerce, Darling. No matter what anybody tells you, romance is a commodity, a multi-billion dollar industry, ripe to be bought, packaged, and sold."

Eric noted the marked contrast between the company's Imaginary Boyfriend figureheads and the dozens of ordinary-looking guys who populated *Virtually Mine's* work force. All across the room, the ordinaries pecked relentlessly at their computer keyboards, even more diligently as their distinctly sultry supervisor approached.

Eric turned to her. "So, Ms. Raznick—"

"It's Sam to you. I insist," she purred, seemingly undaunted by their apparent age difference.

"So, these guys here, they're actors, too?"

Sam demured. "Let's just say it wasn't in the genes for them. They simply facilitate behind the infinitely more marketable facade that insanely good-looking men like you provide."

Samantha glided to a stop at an underling's station. "Eric, meet Charlie Butters, master of my computer domain. Charlie, meet *Virtually Mine's* newest Imaginary Boyfriend, Eric Bender. I need him in the system by day's end."

Eric watched as Charlie's eyes momentarily bugged. The guy had to be smart, he thought. But it seemed that Charlie's merits were hidden under an unremarkable face.

Charlie bit his lower lip skittishly. "Actually, the server has been inexplicably testy; I'm replacing four hard drives, unless the whole network crashes for the third time since lunch, which would pretty much splatter me till at least midnight, but after that—"

"Today, Charlie," Sam pressed, with a don't-trifle-with-me tone.

"Absolutely, Ms. Raznick," Charlie complied. "Today."

As Charlie obediently scurried away, Sam turned back to Eric. "Ready to rattle some hearts?"

Eric assessed the situation thoughtfully. He was accustomed to being in control, particularly with women, and he wanted to get off on the right foot. "Just so we're completely clear: I'm just a face here. No in-person dates, nothing off-color, no contact with me, nothing whatsoever that bleeds into my actual living-breathing life?"

Sam presumed to take Eric's arm, walking him toward her finely-appointed executive office. "Your 'Virtual Girlfriends' won't even know your real name. There's the overall license for your face, plus per client commissions, which you're welcome to drop by and pick up daily. The Operators out there, think of them as my worker bees. They make all the calls. They send cards and gifts, all simulating the Imaginaries' relationships from here."

"And as far as the real love thing goes, it's just an act," Eric confirmed.

Sam just smiled. "Isn't it always?"

Charlie Butters padded over to Samantha's office door and cautiously peered inside. It was like navigating a veritable minefield, he thought, never knowing which step he took could be his very last. As long as he'd worked at *Virtually Mine*, Charlie had never found a way to get entirely comfortable there, especially not with his femme fatale of a boss. Like always, she knew he was at her door. He could tell. But this seemed to be one of those times that she would force him to initiate. Finally, he gave her executive doorframe a tap.

"Knocking off early?" Samantha hardly looked up from her computer.

Charlie buckled. He always did that when an attractive woman spoke to him, even more so with his boss, the woman who held the purse strings to his meager existence. She was the kind of woman his father had preached many a Sunday sermon about, warning of the perils for those who fell prey.

"Well, I got here eleven, no, actually twelve hours ago, Ms. Raznick," Charlie explained. "So...I'm not so much 'knocking off early' but still, I think I need to go."

Unimpressed, Samantha finally looked up. "The new Imaginary fully integrated into the system yet?"

"Eric Bender, you mean. Well... I got this kind of 9-1-1 text from that apartment building I manage, sort of an all-out garbage disposal emergency and—"

"Charlie, you know how jealous I get."

"Yes, yes. But I'm not exactly, you know..."

Samantha preened. She had a way of posturing herself when she spoke to maximize the intimidation factor for Charlie. "Is exclusive the word you're grasping for?"

Sweat beaded on Charlie's palms. He wiped them off on his pants, hoping she wouldn't notice. "Yes. I mean, no... Well, in the employment sense I'm...I'm not even full-time. Not that I wouldn't like to be exclusive—uh—or full-time, that is."

"Don't need another full-time computer guy, Charlie," she intoned. "I just need your completely undivided attention during the two-point-five days a week that you're here."

Charlie's mind raced. For months, he'd been trying to work up the nerve to have a serious conversation about his prospects with the rapidly expanding company. Time after time, he'd waited for the right opportunity and now that stomach-turning moment had arrived. Charlie attempted to swallow the hairball in his throat. He took a step into the office, his desire for privacy barely outweighing his abject terror of venturing into her space.

"I could maybe...eventually even quit my day, I mean, night job managing if you'd... It's not like I aspire to unstop toilets or chase down rent. I could be, like, an Operator, maybe...get some more hours."

Ah. It was out there. Finally. And the world hadn't even come to an end. Yet.

Samantha looked up. She scanned Charlie from his discount store tennis shoes to his ordinary bespectacled face. "Really. An Operator. Servicing imaginary relationships."

Reflexively, Charlie began to back out the door. "You know what? Forget I even..."

"Ever had a girlfriend, Charlie?"

Charlie thought back. Nothing. He reached back farther. "Well, in tenth grade there was this one girl that—"

"Ever been in love?"

Charlie's expression changed as he considered the question. He realized that he had been very much in love. Then, just as suddenly, Charlie's brow furrowed with uncertainty. "With somebody? You mean at the same time as that person was in love with me?"

Samantha nodded. "Mm-hmm." She had a talent for making Charlie feel just as absurd as he realized he sounded.

His face fell. "Then no," he admitted.

Samantha studied Charlie for what seemed an eternity, never breaking that penetrating gaze of hers. It seemed to pierce right through him, like she had some kind of sci-fi superpower. "You've never been with a woman. Have you?"

For the first time, Charlie straightened his back defensively. "Now, see...here's the thing about that. I'm pretty sure a, uh, response to that is not—due respect of course—it isn't a prerequisite for permanent full-time legitimate hire. And please, please assure me that this company is completely and entirely legitimate, because I already promised my dad that it was."

Samantha smiled knowingly. "You've never even pursued a woman, have you?"

Charlie shifted on his feet. It wasn't a subject he relished talking about, especially at work. "See, I've really been planning to, I just—"

She sat back. She massaged the nape of her neck, continuing to assess him. "Plenty of pent-up unrequited emotion to draw from. Over a decade of latent longing... Okay."

Charlie's eyes widened. "Okay?" As soon as he'd asked, he realized that he shouldn't have. He knew that Samantha Raznick was not a woman to repeat herself. When she'd made up her mind, that was that.

"You've got two weeks," Samantha allowed. "Tech maintenance is still priority, but you can try operating for the balance to thirty hours. Pull your weight and I bump you to full time, after which I would, of course, expect you to dump the apartment managing job."

Charlie couldn't believe it. "You won't regret this," he promised, still trying to convince himself that she wouldn't.

"Stirring ardor toward your comelier female counterparts can exact a personal toll," Samantha warned. "So, when it comes to regretting this decision, the question is: Will you?"

Kate pulled her jacket closed as she hurried along the block to Dustin's bungalow. The sun had gone down, but the night air wasn't the only thing giving her a bit of a chill.

Over dinner, M.J. had said something that kept rattling around in Kate's head. She had floated a not-so-subtle hint that Kate could do better than Dustin. Kate never saw herself as being better than anyone else, so she had quickly risen to Dustin's defense. Sure, Kate was aware of their differences, but Dustin was still a great guy. She liked to think how their strengths and weaknesses balanced each other out and made them an even better couple.

As she walked along, Kate thought about the many ways that Dustin had found a place in her heart. He was sweet and playful and fearless. He was always calling, popping with ideas for fun things that they could do. Dustin had given her a sense of belonging there, something she really appreciated whenever she got homesick. Mostly, she thought about how he'd encouraged her to get past her doubts and have faith in herself. So, it seemed only fair that she should set her worries aside, and have a little faith in him, too.

Determined to prove M.J. wrong, Kate knocked on Dustin's door. His bungalow was a tiny place—one room with a postage stamp kitchen and a bath. She'd helped him find it and fix it up a bit with garage sale chic.

"Coming!" Dustin called from inside. It was reassuring to hear his voice. At least it was till he opened the door, and a quizzical expression crossed his face. "Kate, hi. Didn't we say we weren't going to work tonight?"

"You did, " Kate started, "but I was thinking... I just...ahh... Okay, forgive the sentence fragments, but cards-on-the-table here. Maybe I just thoroughly read this wrong, so tell me if I'm just spaced, but is there any chance... Are you thinking you want to see other people?"

Dustin leaned in, a look of confusion on his face. "What...do you think we should?"

"I don't," Kate clarified. "But with today and the whole thing with Wissy..."

Checking behind him, Dustin quickly closed the door and whispered, "Oh! Right, right. I meant to tell you. Soon as she gets me going with this casting director, I'm totally passing the favor on to you."

Following Dustin's train of thought could be challenging. As endearing as he could be, he wasn't the crunchiest chip in the bag. "Dustin, why are you whispering?"

"Because Wissy's here. We're gonna rehearse," he explained with an innocence that Kate knew extended well beyond his ability to act.

"She's here?!" Kate blurted. The words came out just as Wissy opened the door carrying two wine glasses in one hand.

"Oh. Hi, Kate," Wissy leaned coyly toward Dustin. "Dusty—now, what do you think? I brought red or white. I know it's going with salmon, but I don't mind breaking the rules."

"Red's great," Dustin replied.

With that Wissy waltzed back in toward the kitchen. "Almost ready," she cooed.

Dustin turned back to Kate. She could see that, clearly, he wasn't getting it. "She's cooking for you?"

"Yeah, great, huh?" Dustin beamed. "Love salmon."

"And she brought wine? Dustin, this is a date," Kate protested.

"No, it's not," Dustin insisted. "It's not a date unless a guy says it's a date, and I promise. I didn't say that. This is work. And I told you I've got to get at least some kind of something going on with her if the scene's going to fly."

Unable to mask her fears, Kate pressed. "That would be the rampantly gaga, smash-face scene you were going to do with me?"

Dustin tipped his head. He always did that when things weren't quite computing. "Kate, I'm really starting to wonder about you. I mean, I can handle this acting thing. But you... You really gotta learn to split the personal stuff from the work."

Kate absorbed his words, incredulous. "I need to... You think I..." She shook her head in disbelief. "You know what? You're right. Maybe we should see other people because, no, I can't handle this. You want to go *work* with Wissy? Then go ahead. Do what you have to do. Why let the good thing we've had going for the past three months stand in your way?"

Grinning broadly, Dustin grabbed Kate for a stunningly oblivious hug. "Thanks, Kate! I knew you'd be cool with this." With a wave, he hurried back inside and closed the door.

Crushed, Kate just stood there staring. Hot tears sprang to her eyes as she finally replied, too softly for Dustin to hear. "Who said I was cool with this?!"

There was something about ice cream that had always comforted Kate growing up. It reminded her of happier times, when she and her Mom would walk to the Crozet Mennonite dairy where they churned five different flavors by hand. Kate's choice would always depend upon her mood, a pattern Kate's mom had pointed out to her. When things were going great, Kate would pick strawberry. She'd congratulate herself with butter pecan or peach. But now and again, there were those times when nothing consoled her like the heaviest artillery of all: full-fatted chocolate.

It had been months since Kate had eaten ice cream. She'd sworn off dairy, in fact. Still, three thousand miles from that Mennonite store, Kate reached into the freezer case at her Santa Monica grocer. It wasn't exactly the same, but it would have to do. Kate pulled out a pint of Rocky Road and closed the door. Her mind wandering to visions of whatever sizzling dish Wissy was serving up to Dustin, Kate reopened the freezer case and switched the pint for two half gallons.

Wearily, Charlie approached his apartment door. Taped under the *Manager* sign was a folded note that said: *Charlie...Help!!!* It was signed, *Mrs. Teasdale, apartment 305* (as if Charlie's memory were every bit as challenged as his somewhat eccentric tenant's).

Mrs. Teasdale was never shy in her usage of exclamation points, or about expecting help far above and beyond the normal duties of an apartment building manager. Whether her roof was caving in, she'd heard some noise, or if she'd just forgotten how to reset her clocks, the widow Teasdale was an equal opportunity punctuator.

Sometimes, it seemed that Mrs. Teasdale was just lonely. So, Charlie went and sat with her when he had time. Charlie knew what it was like to be lonesome, and besides, visiting older folks was another one of those things his dad had always encouraged him to do.

So, visit Mrs. Teasdale, he did. As her cats popped their claws on her furniture unhindered, he'd help her find whatever was lost in her all too cluttered apartment. There was an up side to visiting Mrs. Teasdale, Charlie realized. She'd serve him chamomile tea and ginger snaps, then chatter his dateless Saturday nights away.

Charlie inserted his key and opened his apartment door. There were three additional notes that had been shoved underneath. Two more were from Mrs. Teasdale, looking much the same as the first. Charlie's heartbeat went double-time when he saw that the third note (with nary an exclamation point) was from his next-door neighbor. All it said was:

So sorry to bug you at work. ~ *Kate*

She'd buttoned the message with a conciliatory smiley face, the lips drawn kind of crinkly in the middle before curling up at the ends. In the seclusion of his bachelor apartment, Charlie ran an affectionate finger across the spot where Kate had written her name.

"You don't bug me, Katie," he murmured, a soft smile on his lips. "Well, you do...but not at all in a bothery kind of way."

Kate slumped on the sofa, numbly downing ice cream with a tablespoon, straight out of the carton. She'd read that chocolate had a mood elevating quality, but the more she ate, the worse she ached. The phone rang repeatedly, but Kate couldn't bring herself to pick up the call. She just stared, even when she heard her mother's voice, leaving a message.

"Hi, Sweetie. Daddy and I are going to bed, but I'm just so happy for you and Dustin and I thought maybe I'd catch you in."

"Hi, Baby," Kate's dad, Wally, chimed in from the background.

Her mom's voice broke a bit. She finished her message half giggling. "Yeah, sorry we missed you, but—Wally! Wally, quit. You know how kids hate to hear this kind of thing! Let me just—" Her mom barely returned her attention to the call. "Anyway, Honey, nightie night!" A torrent of laughter from both followed, long before the truncated phone call disconnected.

Kate's parents had that wonderful kind of relationship, still playfully amorous after all these years. Usually, Kate found these peeks into their love life encouraging. They had exactly what she wanted, no doubt. But on this particular night, their togetherness only hammered home how dejected and alone Kate already felt.

M.J. emerged from her room, her arms piled high with laundry. "You gonna be okay while I'm out?"

Kate removed the spoon from her mouth and stuck it into the ice cream carton with a sigh. "Yeah, I've got, like, a jillion fat grams here to keep me company." She tried to smile, though tears streaked.

Balancing her load precariously, M.J. opened the door to leave, just as Charlie had his hand raised to knock, a toolbox in tow.

M.J. checked Kate's mood warily, and then turned back to Charlie. "Charlie, hi. Maybe it's not the best..."

Charlie looked past M.J. to Kate's tear-stained face and quickly sized up the situation. "Is this a bad time? It's a bad time."

"Well..." M.J. began.

"No, come in, Charlie," Kate managed. "We need the sink back."

M.J. flashed Kate an 'a*re you sure*?' glance.

"I'm fine," Kate retorted. "Look at me, how fine I am."

Entering, Charlie stopped in his tracks. Seeing the ice cream, Charlie whispered to a departing M.J. "Is that dairy? That's dairy."

With that, Charlie spun to leave, but M.J. was too quick for him. She soundly pushed him back inside, just before she scooted out and closed the door.

Suddenly alone with Kate and completely unsure how to behave, Charlie slinked past her, toward the kitchen, filling the awkward air the best he could. "I'll just... Trust me. You won't even know I'm here. It's an extraordinary facility I seem to have with...all women, actually."

three

Under normal circumstances, unstopping a garbage disposal wasn't as engaging a task for Charlie as it was on this particular night. It wasn't so much about the mechanical challenge that the job presented as it was the opportunity it afforded for time with this specific tenant.

Charlie wasn't given to crushes. He knew they were an exercise in futility. But from the moment M.J. had brought Kate in as a roommate, something had done somersaults inside of Charlie. It happened every single time he saw or thought of her.

Kate wasn't a fashion plate. She didn't have the kind of beauty that got applied every morning and washed down the sink at night. Kate was just girl-next-door, fresh-scrubbed pretty. Unlike most girls Charlie met, Kate actually looked him in the eyes when she talked to him. She'd ask about his day, then stop to listen. She said please and thank you when she requested his help. She let him walk with her to church, since Dustin had to work.

Charlie had known Kate was taken from the very beginning when Dustin had helped her move into her so-near-yet-so-far apartment next door to him. It's not that Charlie found Dustin to be worthy of Kate, but he reasoned it was just as well since he didn't deem himself worthy of her either.

Kate was the girl of Charlie's dreams, this marvel of a creature who sat on the counter to the right of where he worked on his back, underneath the sink. As he cleared the culprit cucumber peelings from the garbage disposal trap, she vented the pains of her unexpected break-up, dangling her shapely calves from her perch, driving his besotted soul berserk.

"How can that not turn personal," she asked, not really waiting for an answer. "He's human. He's wired to respond to sensory stimuli. And an acted kiss—I don't care what anybody says. It's still in the same physical universe of kissing."

Conversation about kissing was almost too much for Charlie in this company. He sat up too quickly and bonked his head.

"You know what it's like," she assumed.

Charlie did not. Here he was, a grown man of twenty-seven, living in the big city, and he'd never once in his life kissed a girl, except for his mom and his great aunt Cecelia, neither of which he figured should count.

Kate went on, elaborating every detail of what Charlie had never experienced. "Your mouth gets all tingly," she described, "and your hormones go completely wha-ho! And even if it is in a technical sense *work*, it still pushes exactly the same chemical buttons inside. Whether you claim you're acting or not, a kiss is a kiss. Don't you think?"

Kate hopped down. She paced opposite the sink where Charlie busied himself with her garbage disposal. From his vantage point under the sink, he had to fight not to watch her willowy legs as they passed. They were just legs, he told himself. He had seen legs before, just never from this exact angle.

"What do you think they're doing right now?" Kate asked.

"Well, I..." Charlie blustered, "I try not to think about those kinds of things, things I can't—"

Kate stopped pacing. She leaned back against the counter. "You're right. Why am I torturing myself? I should just focus. Think about...I don't know, I should conjugate verbs or contemplate asparagus or—"

"Sometimes I think of pi," Charlie interjected, understanding the feeling.

Kate seized on the suggestion. "Back home in Virginia, my Mom makes the best pie. It's this apple custard with little bits of apricot jam dotted in it. I'm telling you, Charlie, there's not a sweeter thing that could ever touch your lips."

Charlie felt himself going even paler than he normally was. In fact, he came close to passing out altogether. "I was thinking of the mathematical kind of pi, solving it, but—" Charlie tried to scoot out from under the sink smoothly, but he banged his head soundly on the cabinet frame. "Ow-ow-ow," he yelped, before he could stop the words from exiting his mouth. He'd always felt like something of a doofus, but never more than at that very moment.

Kate peered under the sink. "Charlie, are you okay? Let me look."

Kate's close proximity only increased Charlie's anxiety. She brushed the hair back off his brow. "Hold still. Lemme see."

Charlie winced. "It's only a little...blood and—"

Kate examined Charlie's scalp. "You sure? I could put some ice or...we don't have ice. How about ice cream? Ice cream might work."

As quickly as he could, Charlie rose to his feet. In fact, he rose so quickly that he made himself woozy. "That's okay. I should... You look good...I mean, the disposal looks really...good, now, and I'd better go." With that, Charlie hurried out.

It wasn't that Charlie wanted to leave Kate. He craved every moment of any and every excuse to be in her presence. But there was something about this conversation that had escaped his control. It had been more challenging to his constitution than he'd ever before experienced with Kate.

So, as much as Charlie wanted to stay, he knew he should go, before he said or did anything to overstep his self-imposed bounds or to embarrass himself more thoroughly than he already had. He needed a bathroom, his bathroom, and he needed it just as soon as was physically possible.

Blocks away at the neighborhood Fluff & Fold, M.J. toted an armful of wet Meter Maid uniforms toward an open dryer. As she stooped to pick up a renegade sock, an elderly man and wife toddled past. They took the last open dryer, right out from under her.

"Oh, look, Honey, here's one," the woman beamed.

"Actually, I was going to use..." M.J. sighed. There was no way she was going to wrestle the dryer away from that sweet old couple. Instead, she put her wet wash down and plopped into a plastic chair. "I'll get the next one," she said, as nicely as she could muster.

Missing M.J.'s nuance completely, the woman chattered merrily to M.J. as she loaded their clothes into the dryer. "You know, we met sixty years ago, right in this Laundromat. I was waiting on a dryer at the time, just like you."

"Were you, now?" M.J. replied with more enthusiasm than she felt. As the old woman nattered on about their story, M.J.'s mind drifted. She glanced out the window just as a dog walker stopped out front to untangle the leashes of the five pooches in her charge.

"There he came," the matron continued, "right through that door. I'm telling you I would have missed him entirely if I'd gotten into that dryer when I wanted it. Good Lord slowed me down, though, let me see what I was supposed to see." She patted her husband's back. "Haven't missed a Tuesday night here since, have we, Dear?"

"Nary a one," her husband replied. "Just goes to show, the bug bites and love can grow from just about anywhere." As the old man started the dryer, his wife leaned in for a squeeze. "Who knew the Fluff & Fold could be so romantic?" he chuckled.

M.J. took the couple in. Her parents had hardly been models of affection, toward her or toward each other. It made her want better than they had ever had. M.J. turned her gaze outside, where the dog walker resumed her duties.

Suddenly, an idea struck M.J. She forgot about losing her dryer. She tuned out the elderly couple. All she could see was that dog walker heading down the sidewalk, behind that band of canines.

Watching intently, M.J.'s wheels turned. This idea had possibility written all over it.

Dustin sat on his sofa, half leafing through the pages of a scene and half monitoring Wissy in his kitchen. With a confident smile, she kicked off her shoes and picked up the wine bottle. Dustin waved her off, showing her his half-full glass. "Thanks, I'm good."

Wissy eased herself onto the cushion beside him. "I suspected that."

"What?" Dustin asked, not really getting it.

"That you're good...at whatever it is you do." Wissy put the wine bottle down and cozied up to Dustin, looking over his shoulder at their scene.

Dustin scooted away a bit and handed Wissy her own copy.

Wissy accepted the pages. "I was thinking we should just jump right into character, see where it takes us."

Dustin wrestled with what to do. He thought about Wissy's new job in casting and the career opportunities she offered. Then, he remembered what Kate had said. "We don't have to do the whole kissing part yet. I mean if you're—"

Wissy moved away. She tossed the scene aside and stood. "Maybe an exercise would help. Ooh. I have one. We're going to speak to each other without words."

"We are?" Dustin stymied as to how that was even possible.

"Go ahead, Sweetie," she coaxed. "Stand up."

Dustin stood a few feet away, but Wissy waved him closer. "Come as near as you want, feel the chemistry building for the scene, but resist actual contact."

Confusion clouded Dustin's mind. "Don't touch you?"

"Let me show you," Wissy offered. "Turn around."

Dustin pivoted, not altogether sure what to expect. From behind Dustin, Wissy moved her hands slowly around his face and neck, millimeters away, never grazing him.

She whispered softly into his ear. "If we do it right, we should be able to unearth what these characters are feeling without even so much as the slightest physical brush. We just light the match under it, let it simmer a little, disturb the molecules as they say and... Do you feel that?"

With Wissy's warm breath and the sound of her sultry voice in his ear, Dustin's resolve fell as his temperature rose. "This is an excellent exercise," he pronounced. "I'm just a little...whoa...okay..."

"You're not nervous about this, are you?" Wissy teased. "Come to think of it, maybe you're right. Maybe we shouldn't rehearse the kiss. Maybe we should let everything we're feeling here compound, right up until the actual performance."

The next day felt like a corner turned as Kate poured coffee for regulars at her day job. The Doo-Wop Dinette was a kitschy kind of "Mom and Pop" eatery that had been part of the Santa Monica landscape for generations. Petitions had saved it as a landmark when it was threatened for demolition. Fifties music and throw-back uniforms completed the theme.

Kate had been grateful to Dustin for getting her hired to work alongside him there, but given their exchange from the previous night, she felt unsure just how to behave. She wondered if she should try to act normal, as if nothing had happened, but that didn't feel right to Kate. Something had definitely shifted between them and she had no idea what more to say than what she already had. What she knew for sure was that she needed her job to pay her bills, Dustin or no Dustin.

Mercifully, Kate was on the sunrise team that week. After a sleepless night, she'd been up before dawn, at it for hours before Dustin coasted in for second shift. Careful to avoid his notice, Kate watched Dustin as he trailed the head waitress. At forty-five, Reesa Davis was a straight shooter with a heart of gold, very at home in her plus-sized body.

"I promise, Reesa," she heard Dustin plead. "I'll be gone an hour, ninety minutes tops."

Reesa studied Dustin with a skeptical look on her face. "Didn't you just get here? Kate's off in ten and I've been slinging hash since the birds woke up."

"I wouldn't ask if it weren't, okay, the absolute biggest break so far in my entire career," Dustin justified.

Reesa chuckled. "Uh-huh. And just what is this commercial for?"

Filling sugar jars nearby, Kate bent an ear toward the conversation

Dustin's shoulders bobbed. "Some kind of cold stuff."

Reesa drew back in her inimitable style. "Sneeze medicine? Baby, if this is as good as you got, then far be it from me to stand in your way."

Overjoyed, Dustin planted a wet one on Reesa's cheek. "Thank you, thank you, thank you!"

Reesa chortled with a nod toward Kate. "Best stop that kissin' on me, now. You're gonna make that girl of yours jealous."

Kate averted her eyes as Dustin glanced over at her, but she overheard his reply to Reesa.

"Yeah, we sort of, well..." Dustin shuffled. "She brought it up that we should see other people."

Dinette cook, Andre, rang a bell and placed a steaming plate of spaghetti and meatballs on the pickup counter. He called to his wife, "Order up!"

Reesa whirled to Andre congenially. "I got ya, Cup Cake. No need to go mashin' that bell."

Gathering up her courage, Kate approached Dustin, who was already removing his apron. "Hi," she managed. Awkwardly, he returned the greeting.

Kate struggled for a way to break the ice. She followed Dustin toward the staff locker room. "So, I'm sorry I interrupted your...rehearsal."

Dustin opened his locker, oblivious to the elephant in the room. "No problem."

"You going somewhere?" Kate already knew the answer, but she still had to ask. It was the only way to keep the conversation going.

Dustin bubbled over with excitement. "Okay. Try to remain calm. Wissy called me this morning and she said she's already getting me in on a national commercial."

Kate didn't know whether to be thrilled or devastated. "Really?"

"I'm not on the official list," Dustin continued, "but she's working the session and she says she'll let me crash if I can get over there in the next thirty minutes, so—"

Kate shook her head. "I thought you said she was an intern to an assistant to a semi-monstrous sized casting director."

"Who is slumming in commercials in between, where I can meet her, I know! How do I look?"

Kate tried her best to hold it together. "Like a waiter?"

Dustin began to unbutton the shirt of his uniform. "Doesn't matter. It's shirtless."

Kate watched as he took the shirt off and hung it in his locker. "Shirtless. Great, of course. Then you're... Great. Just great."

There were times when Dustin could be completely nonsensical and this was certainly one of them. For an actor, he had very little grasp of nuance. He didn't seem to get what was being said between the lines, what Kate wished to heaven he could hear without her having to come right out and say it. Instead, Dustin grinned broadly, accepting her words as a compliment. He turned his bare back to her and ambled out the door.

four

In the privacy of his sparsely decorated, one-bedroom apartment, Charlie painstakingly labeled a stack of color brochures. The leaflets were every bit as slick as the company they advertised: *Virtually Mine*. Neatly, he affixed a sticker that said "Operator 52" to each one. Charlie lined each label up as straight as he could, right beside the contact info, wanting it to look as legitimate as possible. After all, he reasoned, he was finally a bona fide Operator for the company and he wanted to do a good job.

Charlie opened one of the brochures. He studied its offering of Imaginary Boyfriends for lonely-hearted souls desiring a sense of beau-like companionship and attentions. The Imaginaries pictured were a variety of ages and types, but every one of them, in his own way, was just as insanely good-looking as Eric Bender had been. There were chiseled jaws, broad shoulders, and perfect hairlines straight across the board. There wasn't a single unstraightened, unwhitened tooth in the bunch.

Charlie looked into the mirror, examining his reflection in contrast. It's not that he was bad looking, but he knew he was no Eric Bender. That was for sure. Charlie had never given much thought to his average, boy-next-door looks. With his dark hair and brown eyes, he was the spitting image of his father, something that had delighted his dearly departed mother to no end.

Maybe I should get contacts, Charlie thought. He took off his glasses to check out the change, but quickly put them back on, unable to see himself without them.

Charlie cracked the door of his apartment and peeked out. The coast was clear.

He sneaked door-to-door, hanging one of his *Virtually Mine* brochures on each knob, even Mrs. Teasdale's.

Circling back to Kate's door, right next to his, he checked around. There was still no one to be seen. Surreptitiously, he dangled a brochure on Kate's doorknob, then whispered heavenward:

"Okay, I know in the tenth grade I told you I was putting the whole chimichanga on Gina Paphites, and I'm not saying I'm faulting you for not coming through for me on that one, but...okay, this once... Just—"

Suddenly, M.J. opened their apartment door. Charlie whirled.

"Charlie, hi!"

"M.J! You're not—"

"Littering Santa Monica with parking tickets? Yeah, I...took a personal day. Check out what I just made." M.J. flashed a computer-generated business card. It read:

No time to walk your favorite pooch? Just Call:
M.J. Poster, Dog Walker Extraordinaire!
310/555-6243

"Okay," M.J. went on, "I get that there are pet limits in this building, but it's totally a house-calls thing. So, what's all this?"

Charlie panicked, realizing that M.J. had noticed the brochures saw in his hand. "Me? What, you mean these? I... Well, you know those pesky solicitors, always selling some new something or other. Yesterday it was botox coupons, today it's..."

Charlie looked at the brochures. "What are these, anyway? Because I'm just, sort of, collecting them—in my capacity as...manager—picking them up, so all of you residents don't have to be bothered with recycling them."

With that, Charlie reached for the brochure on the knob to Kate and M.J.'s apartment. He buckled as M.J. snagged it up first, then tossed it into the apartment and closed the door.

"I got it."

"Okay," Charlie replied. "So...I'll consider yours...disposed of in a completely eco-friendly manner."

"Yup. Bye." And with that, M.J. headed away.

Charlie looked back at Kate's apartment door. He glanced back at the brochures he'd hung on the other doors. "Bye! I'll just grab these last few..." Charlie trailed behind M.J. as she left, taking brochures off of all the remaining doors where he'd just hung them, knowing that the only one he cared to hear from was Kate. "There. Got it. That's done."

Hyperventilating, Charlie waved at M.J. as she rounded the back corner to the parking garage, his mission accomplished.

Back at the Doo-Wop Dinette, Kate dressed salads as Reesa poured iced teas nearby. As it turned out,

Kate had decided to cover for Dustin. It gave her the chance to vent about what had just happened to Reesa's understanding ears.

"I can't believe he told you that I brought it up that we should see other people," Kate sighed.

"I'd say he believed it, too," Reesa nodded. "All due respect, but the boy is not that good an actor."

Kate wiped a spill off the counter. "Well, I said the words, more like a facetious question to him, which he wasn't supposed to answer 'yes' to, much less flip it around on me."

Reesa chuckled. She grinned like she always did when she was about to confide about some juicy tidbit from her wealth of marital experience. "You know what I did, way back when that slippery Andre over there was trying to shuffle the deck?" Reesa nodded discreetly toward her husband of fifteen years, the cook behind the counter.

Intrigued, Kate stepped closer. "What? Tell me."

Reesa lowered her voice. "I got me this fine looking cousin, uhm-hmm. I got him to parade 'round on my arm, like we was some kind of wailin' hot thing. Not two shakes before Andre come runnin' to ask for my hand."

A sea of actors filled the lobby outside half a dozen audition studios within a large casting co-op. Men in suits prepped lines around one door, cheerleaders practiced moves around another, grannies flanked the third, little people the fourth, and bikers the fifth.

Still shirtless, Dustin passed by them all, enjoying the attention his washboard abs drew. Nearing the sixth casting studio, Dustin checked the board for the product listing. It was right there, just as Wissy had said it would be, but oddly enough, all of the guys waiting nearby were wearing shirts.

Dustin didn't let it bother him. He knew he'd followed Wissy's instructions. Besides, he never minded when he attracted attention. He told himself how impressed Wissy would be when she saw how committed he was to booking this gig.

Wissy popped out of Studio Six with a camera. "Eric Bender," she called.

Immediately, Eric rose from his seat.

"Against the door," she directed.

Dustin watched as Eric stepped into place and, with his face at a jaunty tilt, winningly smiled for the camera.

Dustin wished that this Eric guy hadn't been so good looking. In fact, as Dustin glanced around at the men who were waiting, his confidence began to wane. The thing was, Dustin was used to being the best looking guy in the room. He thought of himself as a solid eight and a half. The problem was, in this particular room, he was surrounded by stone cold tens.

Wissy snapped the shot and handed Eric the photo that her camera spat out.

"Thanks," Eric said. "How we doing for time?"

Wissy checked her watch. "Slammed. But I'll squeeze you in." With warm familiarity, she stroked his arm.

As Eric moved off, Dustin sidled up to Wissy. "Hey..."

Wissy took a gander at Dustin's physique. "Wow. Somebody's been working out. Okay, don't hate me, but I totally forgot to text you. It's nice casual now. You did bring a shirt, right?"

Dustin did his best to cover the fact that he did not. "Oh. A shirt. Right."

Wissy turned to address the group of waiting auditionees. "Okay, listen up, now. Jean-Luc, Brent, Adam, Carlos...you're up." Shirted hunks rose compliantly.

Dustin searched around in desperation. He stopped a guy in an open oxford over a v-necked tee. "Dude, can I bum one of your shirts?"

"Sorry," the guy replied. "I always book with this layered look. It's my trademark."

Dustin whirled to a man passing by in a suit. “Hey, you got an undershirt you could loan me?”

“What, are you nuts?” the man asked.

Dustin’s eyes fell back on Eric as he sat on a bench waiting. “I’ll give you ten bucks for your shirt, man.”

Eric looked up, bemused. “Gee. Hundred dollar custom made in Italy. Tempting, but no.”

Just then, Wissy called out over the crowd. “Okay, Eric, Miguel, Ted, and Dustin. You’re on deck.”

Hearing Wissy call his name, Dustin searched around more frantically than ever. He found himself surrounded with white-haired grannies in pastel sweaters. Beyond them were the bikers, the little people, and the cheerleaders.

What in the world could he do?

Minutes later, Dustin entered the casting studio for his very first big audition. As it turned out, he found that there was no semi-monstrous sized casting director who was slumming in commercials present, at least not in the audition studio. There was only a video camera to record the audition, which he learned would be uploaded and posted online for the clients to view later. They wouldn’t know that Wissy forgot to text him about needing a shirt. He wouldn’t have a chance to explain. What they saw on the tape would have to be enough to set him apart from the rest.

Wissy dutifully lined the men up, training her lens on Eric first. "Tell us your name, into the lens, then show me your hands as I go down the row. And you are..."

"Eric Bender." Eric put both hands up below his face, and then flipped them around for the video camera. Wissy panned left.

"Hi, I'm Miguel Ruez." Dustin watched as Miguel did the same thing with his hands.

Again, Wissy panned. "Next we have..."

"Ted Delaney."

"And last but not least..." Wissy panned to Dustin where he stood at the end of the line, wearing a floral, crocheted granny vest over his otherwise bare chest. Dustin shrugged sheepishly as the camera reached him. He flashed his hands and a toothy grin, making the absolute most of it. "Hey. I'm Dustin. Dustin Hunt."

Charlie snugged his tie up to the collar of his dress shirt. He didn't own much in the way of business attire. Tee shirts were more his normal speed, but this day was different. It was his first day as a

Virtually Mine Operator and he wanted to be seen in an entirely new way.

Nearing Samantha's door, he paused to gather his thoughts. He willed himself to put his shoulders back like his dad always advised. Resolutely, he rapped on her doorjamb.

Samantha rose, a puzzled expression forming. "What's with the tie? I didn't know you owned one."

"I didn't, actually," Charlie stammered, "but I thought since I'll be, kind of, working directly with our clients, now—"

Samantha perched on her desk. "Think about it, Charlie. It's not like we can let the girls actually see you."

Charlie did think about it. He thought about it hard. Suddenly, he slumped, feeling as ridiculous as he realized that he looked.

Still, Samantha gestured him toward the hall. "Let's go get you started."

As a computer tech, Charlie had heard about *Virtually Mine's* storehouse of gift items, but he'd never actually been behind the golden door before. Samantha swiped a card key and motioned Charlie through security.

Inside, an enormous room was filled with huge shelving units, laden with gifts that the company's Operators distributed on behalf of their client's

Imaginary Boyfriends. There were silk bouquets, stuffed animals, jeweled trinkets, and more heart-shaped boxes of candy than Charlie ever knew existed.

Samantha breezed through the well-organized aisles with Charlie. "All right, listen up. I'll say this once. Cards are labeled by alphabetized occasion, 'B' for birthday before 'B' for blanks. Suggested messages for the blank cards are in the software, which, given your manifest lack of savvy in this arena, you should rely upon heavily."

Charlie surveyed the offerings, his breath short. "Right."

Samantha continued, never missing a beat. "Cross reference gift ranks with the corresponding level of payment and log each gift onto the account as you pull it. Do not, under any circumstances, boost levels. Got it?"

Charlie nodded. He totally got it, at least on an intellectual basis. Resolving technical difficulties was one thing, but interacting with actual women as an Imaginary Boyfriend, that would be quite another. Though he did his best to hide his unmitigated fear of rising to this ersatz romantic occasion, his heart beat triple-time at the prospect.

M.J. knew that there were defining moments in life, and for her, this gulpy moment felt like one of them. It was now or never, she coached herself. She refused to live in her never. It was high time that she lived in her now.

She would boldly go where no Meter Maid had gone before. She would follow the adorable rusty-haired guy and his golden retriever away from Palisades Park, and into the posh neighborhood it bordered. Maybe he didn't live there, she supposed. Perhaps he'd only pass through on the way to the many apartment buildings just a few blocks south.

Suddenly, the golden retriever bounded up a flagstone walk toward a stately home. The rusty-haired guy followed, and then let himself in the front door.

M.J. swallowed. "Okay, not at all intimidated." She pulled out her freshly-minted dog walker card. Even with its lightly perforated edges, it looked much more official than she felt. "So, here we go," she said as she turned up the walk to the door.

M.J. lifted the polished brass knocker, then lowered it for two distinct raps. Quickly, she rehearsed as she waited. "*Hi...I'm... You're probably wondering why... Hello... Hey, I was—*"

Mid-rehearsal, the door swung open. There was the rusty-haired guy, not three feet away, smiling at her, even cuter close-up than he had been at a distance.

"Hi," M.J. managed.

"Hi. Do I know you?" said the rusty-haired guy.

"Not yet. I mean, now you do...or, a minute from now or..." M.J. thrust her business card toward him, a little more gingerly than she intended. "I'm M.J. Poster, Dog Barker Extraordinaire."

"Dog barker?"

M.J. snorkled involuntarily. "Did I say *barker*? I meant *walker*, not barker, but still most definitely extraordinaire, at the dog walking. It's my business."

"Full time?"

"Working toward it. That's my home number. I'm just building up the clientele, which is why I'm here because I've seen you around, in the park, strictly in a dog scouting context and—"

The rusty-haired guy gestured back into the house. "You saw Freddie?"

"Freddie?" M.J. inquired. "Oh. Freddie's the golden, right? Freddie's my kid brother's name and we won't even go there, but...what did you say your name was?" Just then, M.J. heard the phone start to ring inside.

"I'm Rob. Rob Galloway. And I'd better get that. Might be one of my patients."

M.J.'s eyes bugged a little. "You're a doctor?"

Rusty-haired Rob nodded. "A therapist. Thanks for dropping by, B.J."

"M.J.," she corrected, as cheerily as possible.

With that, Rob took M.J.'s card, went inside, and closed the big door to the beautiful home.

M.J. whirled, elated. She put a hand to her forehead, and then saluted her victory as she strode away. "M.J. Poster, Dog Barker Extraordinaire!"

Kate shuffled into her apartment. Normally, Kate wasn't a shuffler. She had more of a bounce to her step, but shuffle Kate did on this day. In fact, she shuffled right into the *Virtually Mine* brochure that M.J. had tossed in, onto the floor.

Numbly, Kate picked the ad up and checked her answering machine. The L.E.D. readout was a big fat zero.

No one had called her. Not Dustin, not her mom or dad, not even one of those pesky refinance-your-mortgage type solicitors who hadn't done his homework enough to know that she lived in an apartment.

Kate picked up the remote and flipped on the television. Though she was no more a flopper than a shuffler, she flopped on the couch.

A silver-tongued spokesperson announced the upcoming topic as animated graphics filled the screen: "Next up on LIVE WITH CELESTE: Sensational Singles—How to Find Satisfaction Inside Yourself."

Kate rolled her eyes. She grabbed a journal off the coffee table and uncapped its pen.

There were times when the only solace Kate could find was sitting with her journal. It was a place she could unburden herself of everything she was thinking and feeling, no matter how embarrassing it was to admit to anyone but herself.

Kate turned to her most recent entry. It was from just a few days prior. Doodled in the margins of her enthusiastic detailing of what had been a progressing relationship with Dustin, she had written in his last name with her first. How quickly life could change.

As she turned the page, the talk show guest's commentary captured her attention.

"That's when I finally confronted my reality. I'm pushing the big 3-O," the woman on set said.

Kate looked up at the TV. "My sympathies."

The talk show guest continued, as if in answer to Kate. "I live in L.A. where, like it or not, the male population in my decade is divided thusly: fifty-percent married, twenty percent lazy-butt gigolos, roughly fifteen percent are not of my general persuasion, then ten percent are your basic drippy, I'd never look at them guys, and what's left? Let's face it. Prison romances are highly overrated."

Kate zapped off the TV. Lazily, she breezed through the *Virtually Mine* pamphlet, and then talked back to the silenced set. "Hey, you forgot imaginary. The rest of the guys are imaginary."

Just then, M.J. returned to the apartment, bubbling over with excitement. "He's a therapist and his name is Rob. Do you love that? Dr. Rob Cute-Beyond-Belief-With-A-Dog Galloway. Wouldn't that sound great? It rhymes. M.J. Galloway. Ha!"

Kate looked up, determined not to let her own discouragement drench M.J.'s delight. "How did you meet him?"

"I pitched him on my dog walking business."

"You don't have a dog walking business," Kate countered.

M.J. picked up the *Virtually Mine* brochure off the cushion and perched on the couch by Kate. "Well, I couldn't say I'm a Meter Maid. Everybody hates Meter Maids."

M.J. extended a dog walker card to Kate.

Kate admired M.J.'s indefatigable spirit as much as the computer-made card. "Ooh, slick. So, he has your number, now. Maybe he'll call you."

M.J. perused the *Virtually Mine* flyer. "I've heard about this. Mama! Cute guys. You should totally do it. Things don't work out with Robbie-boy, I might."

"They're not real boyfriends," Kate explained. "They're totally imaginary. See? Rent an Imaginary Boyfriend. It's a virtual romance thing."

M.J. leafed through the pages. "I had an imaginary boyfriend when I was eleven. Jimmy Carmichael. Let me tell you, we were quite the little item."

"It says they send you cards and call you and stuff. Shoot, I'd be happy just to have the light blink at me on the answering machine."

M.J. handed Kate the brochure. "So do it. At least an imaginary guy won't break your heart."

Kate shook her head. "It's not like I'm over Dustin. And let me tell you, my mother is definitely not over him."

A look of shock crossed M.J.'s face. "Haven't you told her?"

"Can't. Not yet. So, maybe Dustin isn't classic marriage material, but I already miss him. I still expect him to come walking through that door."

M.J. shrugged. "So, buy yourself a buffer boy. Bridge the gap." The ringing phone interrupted.

"If it's my mom, don't answer it," Kate said. "I'm not ready to get into this."

M.J. checked their Caller ID. Her eyes widened. "It's him!"

"Who, him?"

"My him," M.J. effused. "Rob Galloway!" With that, M.J. picked up the wireless and happily headed back toward her room. "M.J. Poster, Dog Walker Extraordinaire speaking...Oh hi, Rob. Great to hear from you."

Later that night, as hard as Kate tried to focus on pouring her heart out into the receptive pages of her journal, it was that *Virtually Mine* brochure that kept tugging at her mind. She picked it up and leafed through its offerings one more time. It wasn't so much the concept of having an Imaginary Boyfriend that tickled her thoughts. It was the idea of what the illusion might do to Dustin, especially after what Reesa had said about a little competition bringing Andre to his senses.

Maybe, just maybe, an Imaginary Boyfriend could be more than a buffer boy. Perhaps just the impression of her having moved on would be enough to regain Dustin's attention. Maybe it would revitalize and recalibrate their relationship. She could be truthful in what little she would choose to tell Dustin about it. The rest could be her secret.

Pondering things, Kate couldn't see the harm. After all, this boyfriend would only be a flight of fancy. There was no real person this would actually hurt. There was even a chance it might actually help.

Kate picked up the brochure. She studied at its glossy images and the Internet site it boasted. Clearly, this was a thriving enterprise. A lot of women must be renting Imaginary Boyfriends from them for one reason or another, she presumed. Finally, Kate put the brochure down. Resolutely, she told herself there was no way in heaven that she was anywhere near that desperate.

five

Charlie straightened up in his chair. His new Operator's terminal was perfectly organized. The top of the desk had the faint aroma of disinfectant. It wasn't that Charlie was a germ-o-phobe, but nothing had been happening, so he'd passed the time by wiping down his new station with the antibacterial wipes that had come with his take-out lunch. It couldn't hurt, he had told himself.

Samantha Raznick glided by. "You can't just wait for them to come to you, Charlie. Direct Mail, social network, e-mail, cold call—I don't care—as long as absolutely nobody connects the company with your face. You know how to compensate. You've probably been doing it all your life. Make it happen."

Charlie nodded compliantly. "I did put out some brochures this morning."

Samantha stopped. Her face took on an unnerving sneer. "Some? Charlie, please. The ratio of solicitation to response is roughly ninety-to-one. A good Operator maintains a client base of at least twenty, so twenty times ninety is—"

"Eighteen hundred solicitations to go," Charlie calculated.

Samantha clapped her hands as she moved on. "Chop, chop!"

Charlie looked back at his computer screen, overwhelmed. He turned to his silent phone. *How bad could cold calling be?* No one would even know who he was. He could get his feet wet in total anonymity, at least, under the protective banner of the company's Caller ID.

Charlie flipped through his Operator's Manual to the cold calling copy section. Dozens of sample intros were written out word-for-word. All he would have to do would be to read it and the product would sell itself, one out of every ninety calls, the statistics promised. He cleared his throat to practice. Suddenly, a tone from his computer arrested his attention.

A mechanical voice startled him with an announcement: "*You've got a customer.*"

"I do?" Charlie blustered. "I have a—" Charlie rose to call after Samantha. "I have a customer!"

Samantha turned his way, "Well, then. Set the hook; get her profile and credit card. I'll walk you through the rest."

"Right," Charlie agreed, and then sat down at his station. He clicked on his Instant Messaging box.

The system identified the customer: It was Kate Valentine. His Kate Valentine. The message read: *Operator 52, are you there?*

Charlie paled. He folded his hands and raised his eyes. "Thank you, thank you, thank you," he murmured. "Oh, and please don't let me say anything stupid." Don't over think this, he coached himself. Then, remembering Kate's penchant for grammar, he typed a response: *How may I help you?*

Time elapsed.

Charlie checked his watch. A full minute had passed without a reply, yet there she was, still visible on the line. He wondered if this was as hard for Kate as it was for him. He wanted to reassure her, to tell her how amazing she was, something that anyone worth anything couldn't possibly fail to recognize.

Doink! There it was. The IM delivered Kate's answer: *I'd like to try an Imaginary Boyfriend. I think.*

Charlie gulped. He gulped so hard that his Adam's apple crashed into his too-tight tie.

It was actually happening.

Samantha sat at her executive desk, wordlessly perusing Kate's profile. Charlie spread pictures of numerous Imaginaries out on her desk. He tried to remember if he'd ever stood in her presence so quietly for so long. He felt like he should say something; then, he felt like he shouldn't.

Charlie did his best to reserve judgment about people, but something reminded him that Samantha Raznick really was one of those women his father had warned him about from the pulpit, all during his adolescent years. The good Pastor Butters had preached many a sermon, his gaze often drifting to his only son, especially when he'd read cautionary Proverbs about such femme fatales, their voices dripping with honey as they lured their unsuspecting prey to certain doom.

Charlie shuddered. He reminded himself that Samantha had never once been inappropriate with him, at least not in *that* way. He'd explained to his dad that the company's dealings were strictly above board. But there was still something about the woman at the center of it all that kept Charlie ready to run screaming at any given second.

"So," Samantha finally began, "she wants to make her boyfriend jealous."

Charlie's voice cracked. "Ex-boyfriend."

"Ah, to be young and vindictive."

"Well, not so much to get back at him as to get him back." Charlie spread out the many potential Imaginary Boyfriends' photos that he had pulled. "I was thinking we could go with—"

Samantha leaned forward, ignoring Charlie's attempt to make a selection. "Charlie, do you find this girl to be pretty?

"Yeah," Charlie replied. "She's...incredibly, you know...wow...in that department."

Sam rifled through Charlie's assortment of photos, an uninspired scowl on her face. "You really think a pretty girl is going to go for one of these? Where'd you get them, the putz file?"

Charlie balked. "She did say that personality is the most important factor."

"We all say that, so we won't appear to be shallow." Unceremoniously, she tossed the entire array into the trash. "Go with the new guy. Eric."

Charlie nodded.

He started toward the door, and then turned back. "Don't you think, I mean for her, he's a little, you know—"

"Yummy?"

Charlie wandered back to Samantha's desk. "She's just kind of, that is, she seems to be more the type who'd go for, I don't know. Maybe, the boy next door."

Sam rose to her full height. In her five-inch heels she towered over him. "We are dream brokers, Charlie. Nobody fantasizes over the boy next door. Not unless he looks like this."

She plopped Eric's photo into Charlie's clammy hands. "I recommend that you send something personal first. A card with a snapshot and some kind of gift. That is, before you call her."

Charlie's throat went dry. "I call her?"

Samantha shook her head in a way that pummeled Charlie's confidence. "We're only renting his image. Of course, you're the one who calls her. You supply the actual voice, hopefully a scintilla of personality to pepper it up."

"The voice, right," Charlie acknowledged. "But what if she recogni— What I mean is, what if my voice sounds—"

"Create a character," Samantha replied, her impatience growing. "Go over her specs and be the guy she wants. Look, are you sure you can handle this?"

"Sure. Yeah." The words came out much less convincingly than Charlie had hoped.

"Then handle it," Sam replied as she showed him out the door.

Back at his Operator's station, Charlie sat, sifting through photos of Eric. Clearly, these pictures were intended to look like snapshots, as if taken on the spur of the moment. Truth be told, he questioned how could anyone look so good no matter the situation or angle. Some people were just more photogenic than most, Charlie decided.

Other than school photos only a mother could love and a smattering of candid shots from his growing up years, there were relatively few photos of Charlie in existence. He wasn't really sure if it was because his parents weren't exactly camera bugs or if he didn't provide sufficiently inspirational subject matter. Seeing so many great photos of Eric made Charlie wonder.

There were surfing shots, backyard pics as grill chef at a barbeque, even one with Eric swinging a child in a circle by his arms, just like Charlie used to like to do with the kids at his dad's Sunday School picnics. Kids clamored to Charlie. They didn't care how average he looked. They only cared that he enjoyed spending time with them. What it was about growing up that changed all that, Charlie didn't know. But what he wouldn't give, just once, to spin Kate Valentine around in his arms.

As Charlie perused the *Virtually Mine* stock room's offerings, the options seemed limitless. Kate had only paid for an introductory level Imaginary Boyfriend, so though he was tempted to bump what he sent her to their deluxe level, he dutifully pulled a card from the introductory shelf. Somehow, he would make less into more.

Charlie shivered as he walked through a set of glass doors, into the refrigerated section where a sea of cut flowers were kept fresh. He hadn't seen so many arrangements since his grandmother's funeral. Grandmother Butters had always liked roses, but something in Charlie wasn't sure about roses for Kate. He wandered past lilacs, lilies, sunflowers, and spider mums, stymied by the decision. Birds of paradise were a no-brainer for him. Those things were just plain scary.

M.J. motored around the corner toward Rob's house in her Meter Maid Mobile. Ocean Avenue was nice, but there was just something about turning onto Palisades Drive that felt like a world apart. These were the homes of the Santa Monica elite, the people who'd rather pay off the parking tickets she'd write than bother to move their cars. Manicured shrubs set off handsome landscaping in lawns a dandelion wouldn't dare attempt to invade.

Actually, M.J. liked dandelions. As a child, she'd wiled away many an hour by plucking stems that had gone to seed. Then, she'd blow them to see just how far her breath would carry them, out of her not-so-weed-free yard and into the McCubbin's fastidiously kept vegetable garden next door.

Mr. McCubbin would fume at M.J. He'd complain to her mother when she got off work and threaten to call the Community Covenants cops on them. But there was something about the boundary-crossing puffballs of airborne seeds that appealed to the adventuresome spirit in M.J., no matter how much Mr. McCubbin hated them. It had felt like a small victory every time one managed to steal past his rake and sprout amidst his zucchini squash and lima beans.

M.J. pulled over a few doors down from Rob's house. She checked around furtively, and then began to take off her uniform, under which she sported colorful exercise clothes. With a glance in her rear view mirror, she fluffed her hair and smacked her cheeks pink.

Once inside Rob's home, curiosity got the better of M.J. as she waited for Rob to get his golden retriever from the backyard. She peeked around the downstairs rooms adjoining his foyer, then wandered into a handsome office. Seeing a framed photo on the desk, M.J. flipped it around to take a look. A gray-haired couple stood arm-in-arm, smiling for the camera. Hearing Rob and the approaching click of the golden's claws on the hardwood floor, M.J. hastily put the photo down. It clattered to a fall, but she quickly righted it, just as Rob appeared in the doorway with Freddie.

Rob extended the dog's leash toward M.J. "So, here he is. Just fed and ready to go."

M.J. grimaced, caught resituating the photo. "Oops. I was... This is a really nice place you have here."

Rob gazed around the ample abode. "More than I need at this point. Except the office is good."

"So, you live alone here?" M.J. probed. So far, there had been no sign of a spouse, but she couldn't help asking.

Rob shook his adorable head. "Just me and Freddie for now. I kind of inherited the place from my mom and dad."

M.J. nodded, putting it together. "In the photo."

"Yeah." He pointed skyward. "They're up in—"

"Heaven?" M.J. bit at her lip as soon as she said it. "Sorry. Hey," she joked, "maybe they'll meet my folks. Although, I'm not entirely sure about my dad, to tell the truth. He tended to go for warmer climes, if you know what I mean."

Rob smiled. "I was talking about Washington State. They retired there."

"Oh." M.J. kicked herself. Surely, with all of the scabillions of words there were in the English language, she could find just a handful to say. But all that had come to her was that one conversation-curtailing *oh*.

Rob moved toward his desk. "So, I guess I'd better get some work done."

M.J. found her voice again. "Here? You work here?"

"Mornings, yeah. Which is why I took you up on the whole dog walking thing...so I can, you know, work."

Getting Rob's drift, M.J. moved toward Freddie. The beast loomed much larger up close. "The dog walking, right." M.J. leaned over toward the golden with as much confidence as she could fake. "So, Freddie, want to go for a walk?"

On hearing those words, Freddie jumped up on M.J., pawing her multi-print leggings. Unaccustomed to animals, M.J. straightened up as congenially as possible.

"Down, boy!" Rob commanded. "He knows those words." Rob mouthed *go for a walk*.

"Whoa. Yeah. Okay." M.J. laughed nervously while Rob pulled Freddie off of her. She couldn't help but enjoy Rob's closer proximity. In fact, she could hardly bear to tear herself away.

Rob patted Freddie to sit down on his haunches. "He's kind of a flirt," Rob admitted. "You know, I've had the 'little talk' with him, but he's still such a rake. Plastic bags are in his pouch."

A puzzled expression flew across M.J.'s face. "Plastic bags? Oh! Right. Plastic bags. For the...uh, shall we say...produce." M.J. took hold of Freddie's leash and led him toward the front door. "Okay, we're off."

Rob went back to his desk and picked up a book. "Okay."

M.J. talked Freddie to the door, hoping that somehow he'd understand her words and cooperate. She'd heard that dogs could smell fear, so she did her best to mask the willies she was feeling.

M.J. sneezed.

As it turned out, M.J. realized her anxieties about Freddie were overblown. Her confidence grew as Freddie didn't nip or bark at her. He didn't even pay much attention to her as they walked through Palisades Park. All that the dog remained intent upon was searching for the perfect place to do his doggie business.

Finally, Freddie seemed to be zeroing in, circling a particular plot of interest. Moments later, he broke out of that orbit, took a few steps and found another spot to start yet another circle.

M.J. sneezed again, this time even harder. "Why is this grass more perfect than that grass? Can you explain this to me?" Her eyes started to itch the way they had when she'd once attempted to rescue a puppy.

Suddenly, seeing another Meter Mobile motor by, M.J. checked back to make sure that her parked one was still going unnoticed, knowing her break time was over. She clicked her fingers at the dallying dog. "Time to deploy, Freddie. Let's go."

Business was booming at the Doo-Wop Dinette. Kate had to hustle to keep up, but that was fine with her because it made it less obvious that she was doing her best to avoid any sort of meaningful contact with Dustin.

Kate knew that, eventually, she'd have to figure out how to be in the same room with Dustin again. After all they waited tables together in addition to being part of the same acting class. That was it, she thought. She'd make it an acting assignment to herself. She'd act like she was over him. She'd feign being perfectly fine.

Kate picked up an order and scooted to the side to avoid crashing into Dustin. Frustratingly, he mirrored her move. Again, she awkwardly tried to get out of his way, but his countermove put him right smack into her path again. Finally, he stood still, allowing her to get by. Nothing about this was going to be easy.

Kate saw Reesa accept a floral delivery as she passed by to serve a cheeseburger and fries to a man. Kate set a lunch salad—no croutons, with a light vinaigrette on the side—before his female lunch companion. Croutons were one thing, but why it was that women denied themselves anything beyond rabbit food was lost on Kate at that moment. There was no ring on the woman's finger. She was starving herself for him, Kate supposed. She could only hope that this particular man would prove to be worth it.

Kate caught herself. Despite how challenging it was, she didn't want to get jaded. She didn't want to give up hope on all men just because of what she was going through. Of course, it didn't help to overhear Dustin's nearby table of coquettes, flirting with him relentlessly as he took their order.

"Gotta be from Arizona," one said. "All the cute guys are from Arizona."

Dustin preened. "No, but you're warm. You like your chicken grilled, right?"

"You remember everything, don't you?"

Not to be outdone, another interjected. "My turn. New Mexico."

Dustin reared back playfully. "Ow! Sizzling now, Baby."

Kate inwardly imploded as the girls reacted with delight.

Yet another girl toyed, "Yeah, you give me your number, I'll show you some sizzle."

"Gotta guess it, or no number," Dustin replied.

Kate strode by the table, reflexively intervening. "He's from Colorado. And believe me, I've already got his number." As Kate skulked back behind the counter, she wondered if her face looked as scarlet as it felt. Unmercifully, the flirts continued.

"Colorado! That's what I was going to say!"

"Shut up!" another teased.

Kate pretended not to mind.

Dustin egged the girls on. "No, no, gotta guess it. You'll just have to come back another day."

Kate put an order slip on the wheel and spun it around for the cook. "Andre, can you put a rush on this? And skip the butter, he's vegan."

Andre snatched the ticket. "Two pieces of dry, stick-in-the-throat, whole grain toast comin' up."

Reesa sidled up next to Kate, and then nodded knowingly. "Well, lookee who's back in the game."

Kate let out a sigh. "I know. But does he have to do that right in front of me?"

Reesa planted herself. "I'm talkin' 'bout you, Child. Check it out. Those flowers that just came, they're for you." Reesa directed Kate's view to the register. By it, sat a bouquet of fresh daisies.

An excited glow came over Kate as she drank in the sight of the daisies with their dark green foliage, white-white petals, and sunny centers. She pulled the card out, noticing the *Virtually Mine* logo, a red VM, encircled with a heart, on the envelope.

Reesa leaned close. "Tell Reesa who's seein' other people now."

Even realizing that this bouquet was from her Imaginary Boyfriend, Kate was still impressed. She'd said nothing about daisies being her favorite flowers. That alone gave her goose bumps. She opened the card and was surprised to see that the text had been written in by hand. Shyly, Kate read aloud to Reesa:

I could have sent you roses,
Or the lilacs I passed by,
But I am just a country boy,
And daisies caught my eye.
Yours, Brad

Kate blushed with sheer delight. It was all much more personal than she had expected. She flipped to the enclosed snapshot of Brad. Not only was he charming, he was also goo-gobs of gorgeous. Kate couldn't help herself. She melted at the very sight of him. For a moment, Kate forgot all about Wissy and Dustin, much less his table of flirty customers. Then, suddenly remembering, Kate quickly glanced over to see if Dustin had noticed that she'd received a bouquet. Clearly, he had.

Reesa looked puzzled. "Yours, Brad." Who's Brad?"

Kate glowed with resurging confidence. "Looks like my new boyfriend."

six

Eric Bender waited as Samantha smoothly tore off a *Virtually Mine* check, and then handed it to him with a smile. This being his first paycheck, Eric was more than a little curious at what it would amount to be. Seeing the total, his chiseled chin dropped. "Whoa. And this is on top of the license fee?"

Sam rose from her desk, circling closer. "The lion's share is in commissions. Every time your face is successfully assigned to a new client, your take jumps."

Eric studied the check stub. "How many does this represent?"

Sam perched becomingly on the edge of her desk. "Seventy-eight pitter-pattering hearts by my count. I've been pushing you with the drones."

Eric looked over the workstations at the ordinary guys who kept *Virtually Mine* afloat. He noticed Charlie among them. Somehow, he felt the need to confirm their understanding. "So, I don't have to do anything."

Sam shook her head. Her raven tresses swished side to side, then settled back, perfectly into place. "It's the privilege of beauty. They do the work. You visit me to collect, just as often as your heart desires."

Eric was used to women coming on to him. Whether it was ego or insight, there was no question in his mind about what was going on. It was a hazard he had come to accept of the way he happened to look.

There had been times in Eric's life that he might have let the attentions of a woman as beautiful as Samantha get the better of him. It wasn't that he had moral qualms. It wasn't her age that bothered him. It was just that something told him the shelf life on such dalliances wouldn't be so very lengthy. He decided that he wanted to keep the paychecks coming as long as he possibly could. Giving into Samantha's allures simply wasn't a justifiable risk.

Eric eased back toward the door. "You could always mail my check next time. Or direct deposit, that'd be fine by me."

Sam studied Eric, a smoldering smile on her burgundy-painted lips. "I'm more of a face-to-face woman, Eric. I prefer to press the flesh."

Kate trotted briskly towards her old ragtop convertible, her arm around the bouquet of daisies balanced on her hip. She didn't have to look back to know that Dustin was following her out. She heard him pick up his pace, trotting after her. She also knew him well enough to know that there was no way in the world that he would let this go.

Dustin caught up. "You need some help with that?"

"I've got it."

Dustin passed by, getting between Kate and her car. "Your mom sent them. Right, huh? Is it your birthday?"

Kate let out an exasperated breath. "That's next month and no, she didn't." She opened the car door.

"Then who?"

As nonchalantly as she could, Kate secured the bouquet between the seats. "Just a guy."

Dustin knitted his brow. "A guy-guy?"

"His name is Brad. I met him on the Internet last night and yes, by every applicable definition, he's a guy-guy." Kate attempted to get into her car, but Dustin blocked the way.

"I was going to send you flowers once," he insisted. "I was."

Kate looked up at Dustin, her eyes filling with regret. "But you didn't."

"You know I have no money, Kate."

Kate rolled her eyes. She didn't like to do that much, but she couldn't help herself. "That is so not what this is about. Daisies aren't expensive, Dustin. They're just a few dollars a bunch. We used to grow them every summer all along Mom and Daddy's fence. They make me think of home."

Dustin threw up his hands. "How am I supposed to know that?"

"I guess you'd have to know me," Kate replied.

"I know you."

Kate realized that she had a decision to make. She could let this pass, or she could say all the things that she'd stifled for the three solid months they'd been dating. "What's my favorite color, Dustin?"

Dustin looked at her blankly. "Oh, come on."

"Where did I go to high school? What do I binge on? What's my secret obsession? Who do I admire most?"

"You don't know that about me," Dustin defended.

Kate took a deep breath. "Named Best Looking in your graduating class, Theodore Roosevelt High, Denver. Chose wrestling instead of hockey to protect three years of orthodontia and wound up All State in the process. Your two older sisters, Darlene and Alva, financed your move here out of their day trader earnings, much to the dismay of their twin husbands, Ronny and Johnny Beck, who had earmarked that account for a snowmobile. You're afraid of spiders. You have an oily T-zone. Tattoos weird you out. Your favorite food is marshmallows. Cheap detergent makes you itch, and as far as you're concerned, Jack Black is the finest actor on the planet."

"Well, he is!" Dustin shot back.

"That's not the point!" Kate implored. "It isn't always all about you."

In a flash, Dustin whipped out his dinette order pad and clicked his pen open. "Okay. Fine. Tell me all your stuff. Spill it. I'm listening. Go."

Kate could hardly believe it. "What, you're going to write it down?"

"How am I supposed to remember?"

"I remember yours," Kate countered. "You remember your lines."

"I have to do that! Work is work. Relationships are not work."

Suddenly the veil was lifted for Kate. She saw exactly who and what she'd been fighting for. Something inside her shifted. She finally spoke her heart, realizing she had nothing left to lose. "You know what? I thought I wanted you back. I really did."

Kate got in and started her car as quickly as she could. She threw on her sunglasses, fighting tears.

Dustin persisted. "You can still have me! Come on!"

Kate sped away. In her rear view mirror, she could see Dustin blustering after her.

"You're afraid of spiders, too! Aren't you?!"

It had been the longest two hours in recent memory for Charlie. He'd placed the order for Kate's daisies, and then he'd taken the rest of the afternoon off from *Virtually Mine.* It wasn't as if he could get anything done anyway, not with his mind completely preoccupied with wondering just how Kate had responded to what he had sent on behalf of the Imaginary Boyfriend she'd ordered.

Charlie wished he'd had the nerve to stop by the Doo-Wop Dinette, to have seen Kate's face when the daisies had arrived, but given that he'd never even eaten there before, he decided not to risk it. It was risk enough that he'd used part of his middle name.

He reasoned that Kate would be home soon. He knew she was smart, that she'd keep in mind that this was just lark to help her get Dustin back. Still, he wanted to do whatever he could to mend her broken heart.

Charlie had picked those daisies out special. He wasn't sure why, but as soon as he'd seen them, something inside had said *yes*, daisies were the way to go. Though cards with printed verses had been available, he'd spent some concerted time on the poem he composed to attach instead. Beneath the safe cover of Eric's handsome face as Brad, Charles Bradley Butters had finally found a way to get a little more comfortable with Kate, the way he'd long wished he could be with her in person.

Charlie listened to muzak on his phone, peeking out the front window intermittently to the street. Abruptly, the muzak halted. Charlie sputtered. "Hello, yes. This is Operator Number 52 with *Virtually Mine*. I was calling to confirm the delivery of...Yes, I can hold." The muzak resumed.

Charlie stretched the phone cord to look out front again, just in time to see Kate drive up in her ragtop with the vase of daisies beside her. "Okay.

Nevermi...you can't... Bye." Completely flummoxed, Charlie whirled, wrapping himself up in the cord and pulling the phone's base off the table, which went crashing to the floor.

The moment Charlie had been waiting for had finally come and every cylinder of every impulse within him suddenly started firing. "All right, look normal. Look normal."

Charlie's self-directed pep talk did little to slow his racing pulse. He flung open his utility closet and grabbed for a broom. Of course, it got tangled with the mops and the garden hoe and anything else it could possibly get stuck on as it and every other pole-handled tool in the closet came clattering out.

The broom triumphantly in hand at last, Charlie deliberately paused. He closes his eyes and coaxed himself to relax. He tried to remember what his dad had taught him about just such circumstances. *What was it that he had said? Oh, yes*, Charlie recalled. In situations like this, always remember to breathe. It tended to keep him from fainting dead away.

Charlie scooted outside. He skidded to a stop and, as casually as he could, he began to sweep the walk outside Kate's door. Not a split second later, there she was, climbing the stairs with the bouquet he'd sent on her hip. Charlie swallowed, desperate to moisten his drying throat.

Seeing him, Kate smiled warmly. "Charlie. Hi. Didn't you just do that yesterday?"

"Did I?" he squeaked. "Oh. Well, a clean walk is a happy walk, so... Pretty flowers."

Kate sighed as she unlocked her door. "Yeah. My favorites."

Charlie fought for words to respond. "Dustin trying to make it up to you?"

Kate brushed a flaxen wisp from her eyes. "No, it's just...a teensy bit embarrassing is what it is." Kate paused a moment, then shifted to a more upbeat tone. "Garbage disposal is working great."

Charlie stopped his sweeping. Any praise that proceeded from those plump pink lips made his all but tone-deaf heart sing. "You need anything else, man-wise, I mean manager-wise, you just let me know."

Kate smiled. "Thanks, Charlie. I'm going to go put these down. It's been a hard day."

Charlie nodded understandingly and resumed his sweeping. He found it easier to remain calm around her when he had a task to do—something, anything to keep her simple attractions from driving him absolutely wild.

The second that Kate disappeared into her apartment, Charlie bolted back into his. Safely inside, he clutched his pounding heart.

A pile of tissues around her, M.J. dotted on calamine lotion as Kate entered their apartment with the bouquet. Unsuccessfully, M.J. stifled a sneeze.

With a concerned look, Kate approached her roommate. "Are you sick?"

M.J. gathered her tissues. "Not exactly. Turns out I'm allergic."

"To flowers?"

M.J. hung her head. "Dogs. I mean, I knew I was as a kid, but I thought it was like chicken pox or acne or whatever, and I'd have grown out of it. Come to think of it, I never completely grew out of acne either. A pity, you might think, but it does blend quite nicely with the hives."

Kate wandered toward the sofa. "So, are you going to quit the dog walking business?"

"Heck, no." M.J. popped an allergy pill from its cell pack, and then read over the directions.

"What are you going to do?"

"Mainline allergy caps if necessary. And if that results in daytime drowsiness, gastric distress, or occasional dry heaves—believe me, this guy's worth it."

Again, M.J. sneezed.

"Why don't you just tell him?"

M.J. flopped back on the sofa. "That my mouth turns to mush at the sight of him? That I want to lick the spoon he eats his breakfast from?"

"How about just that you like him?"

"See, you...you could do that."

"You could do it," Kate insisted. "Anybody could do it."

"Anybody with a face like yours and a bod like that and, by the way, where on your thighs did you hide that half gallon of ice cream?"

"M.J., you're beautiful!"

"Uh-uh," M.J. answered. "I'm the crack up, the best bud. I'm the go-to girl for a favor."

Kate sat down by her roommate. "You're a lot more than that."

M.J. shrugged. "I'm okay looking. I know that. But romantically, I have to grow on guys. I have to dig deep, send out tillers and rhizomes, and make myself impossible to get rid of. Face it. I'm the Bermuda grass of eligible women. And I'm almost thirty. Did I mention that?"

A look of surprise crossed Kate's face. "You said you were twenty-five."

"I also lie about my weight. Go figure."

Kate wished she could encourage M.J., but it was hard to know just how to do that. The phone began to jingle in Kate's bedroom, so Kate rose to answer it. "M.J.—the right guy—he's going to notice you."

"Rob is the right guy," M.J. called after her. "He just doesn't know it yet."

Charlie paced nervously, his ear to the phone. Under his breath, he tried out what he might say. "*Hi, Kate...no, she'll...okay...I can do this. I'm from the country, the country boy... I'm... Southern, I'm—*"

Suddenly, he heard that Kate had picked up.

"Hello."

Don't panic, Charlie pleaded with himself. He took on a light twang, making himself more comfy in Brad's confident persona. "Well, hey there Katie, this is Brad. I was hopin' I'd catch you in."

The line was silent for a moment. What Charlie wouldn't have given to have seen Kate's face, but knowing she was on the other side of the firewall their apartments shared would have to be close enough. He glanced at her photo on his computer screen, then down at his phone jack, calculating that they were actually just a couple of yards apart.

"Brad from the...I mean, you're my—"

Charlie didn't want her to have to finish that sentence. The last thing he wanted was for anything about this time he had with her to seem anything less than real. "Is it okay if I call you Katie? I just always loved that name."

"Sure," she replied. "Okay. That's actually what my Daddy calls me, and all my friends back home in Virginia."

"Then Katie it is. Katie and Brad. Has a nice ring, doesn't it?"

Charlie couldn't see Kate's expression, but he could hear the smile curling in her voice. He was glad he'd paid such close attention whenever they had spoken.

"Yeah. You sound so...familiar to me."

Charlie straightened, worried. "I do?"

"Yeah, you sound like almost all of Crozet. Everybody's so warm and friendly there. I had to work to lose my accent, coming here. I'm liable to go back to it talkin' to you."

Greatly relieved, Charlie eased into the country boy persona. "Never met a gerund dropper I didn't like."

Again, Kate paused. "That's... You actually know what a gerund is. This is crazy. Most people don't know this, but I'm a total grammar geek. It's kind of my secret obsession."

"You, too?"

"Yeah. Me, too."

There was always something about washing her face before bed that felt good to Kate, but on this particular night the sensation of the warm water and suds was all the more soothing. She didn't know exactly what was happening inside her, only that something in that satisfying phone conversation had seemed like more than a compensated exchange with an Imaginary Boyfriend. Her mind ran with the prospects.

Brad's picture, Kate knew, was of a real guy. She reasoned that he also knew what she looked like, since he had the real photo she had submitted of herself. Even if he were being employed to call her among his stable of clients, she felt special. She decided that it was somewhere in the remote reaches of possibility that something genuine was at play.

Though they stood at their side-by-side sinks wearing pajamas, Kate noticed as M.J. began to apply eyeliner. "You going somewhere?"

"Nope," M,J. answered. "Just wondering if maybe I should change it up. For Rob. You think?"

Kate toweled her face dry. "I'm probably the wrong person to ask about makeup."

M.J. leaned close to the mirror. "Since you don't need any."

Again, it was hard to know just what to say. The closest thing to cosmetics Kate ever wore was lip gloss, and that was mostly for the sunscreen. "I just mean...I think you look great without it. Any guy you get is going to see you without it eventually anyway."

M.J. capped the eye pencil. "Not if I get the permanent kind." M.J. stretched her mouth open and smeared the liner on her lower lid. She backed away from the mirror, checking the results. "So, are you going to tell me about your call, or do I have to install a bug?"

Even though it was only M.J., Kate could feel a blush rise to her cheeks. "I don't know. He's... It's almost like he's...real."

M.J. sighed nostalgically. "So was Jimmy Carmichael."

"It was the first time I talked to him and it's like...he completely gets me." Kate reached for a towel. "He sends my favorite flowers, he's got the cutest little accent, which you know I love and, okay...guess how he puts himself to sleep at night."

"He names all the prepositions in alphabetical order."

Kate looked at her roommate, agape. "How did you know that?"

"Because that's what you do. He probably got it off your profile."

Kate took M.J.'s suggestion in, more puzzled than ever. "That's what's kind of wigging me. Most of it...I never put it on the profile."

seven

Kate was purposely late for Antonio's class. It wasn't like her to be tardy. By and large, she made a point to be punctual, if not early. But knowing that Dustin and Wissy would be putting up their scene didn't make the idea of showing up at all for this particular class attractive.

Still, there was something that drew Kate to the theater. Whether it was a sense of responsibility or a punishing curiosity, Kate found herself wandering into the darkened space and easing into a seat behind her teacher and peers, just as Dustin and Wissy took the stage, scripts in hand. They waited for Antonio's cue to start.

Dustin shuffled his feet. He looked up at Wissy with a chagrined expression. "I'm sorry," he read.

"I don't mean to... I know that thing that happened between us yesterday, it was unprofessional."

Wissy stepped toward Dustin coyly, playing against the written words. "What were we thinking? We just won't let it happen again. That's all."

Dustin took a step closer. "We should draw boundaries."

"And stick to them."

Dustin brushed a tendril away from Wissy's cheek. "Absolutely."

Ever the coquette, Wissy gazed longingly into Dustin's eyes. "Because, we don't want to let this interfere with our working relationship."

"There's that," Dustin replied, millimeters away from her.

Kate squirmed in her seat at the back of the theater. The innocence of her own portrayal of this character was far from Wissy's take on it. It was one thing for Kate to contemplate what was going on between Dustin and Wissy outside of class, but it was quite another to see it play out right in front of her, sparking like the fourth of July.

Their kiss started softly, and then grew in its intensity. Kate wanted desperately to avert her attention, but somehow, she couldn't help but watch. With each bewildering moment, the knife sunk deeper into her heart.

Mercifully, Antonio cleared his throat to curtail the scene, but Dustin and Wissy continued to kiss, lost in the moment.

Hot tears brimmed in Kate's eyes. Finally, she tore her gaze away, unable to watch any longer.

"Well, then," Antonio interrupted. "Very good." Antonio turned to the class. "Who can tell me why that scene worked?"

"It's the chemistry. Plain and simple," Samantha intoned as she handed another day's pay to Eric. "You've got it with the lens, they imagine it's with them—three hundred fifty-eight of them by last count—all across this nation. I have a proposition for you, Eric."

Eric marveled as he spotted his sizable take, especially since he'd only agreed to this job to fill in the financial blanks between acting gigs. "I'm listening."

"Our license with you is domestic, but my instinct is that you could have global potential."

"As in around the world? That globe?"

Samantha sashayed past her desk toward Eric. "I thought it might be interesting to discuss it over dinner. Say eight o'clock. My place."

Immediately, Eric's radar went up. Everything in him told him this didn't seem to be an entirely business-oriented proposition. "Your place. That might be—"

Sam moved closer, toying with him. "Are you as bored with take-out as I am, Eric? I'll cook."

Eric's mind raced.

Samantha held his gaze, her meaning plain.

Eric cleared his throat, stalling for a way to redirect. "Well, no, actually I...I think I'd rather just keep my position with you...domestic, I guess."

Smoothly, Samantha retreated a bit, completely unruffled. A shrewd expression arched across her brow. "Darling, do you know how many there are of you, how many beautiful faces with underdeveloped talent and sub-par personalities populate L.A.?"

Eric raised his hands apologetically. "Hey, I'm not looking to rankle anybody. I just need this job."

"And you only have it because you are an unknown," Sam reminded. "The minute you become known, you're useless to me. Did you realize that?"

"No, I—"

Samantha waltzed away. "Yes, that's precisely my on-going challenge, to find stupendously good-looking Imaginaries who will never succeed in compromising their value to me by making a legitimate name for themselves."

His ego bruised, Eric's eyes flashed. "Hey, I was into three callbacks on an infomercial last week."

Sam sat. "Was it by any chance for male-patterned hair loss? They must have noticed that you're thinning."

Eric self-consciously fingered his temples. "I have a naturally high forehead."

"So did Ray Cooley," Sam retorted.

"Who?"

Sam smiled tightly, her gloves off. "My point exactly. The clock is ticking on your marketability, Eric."

"It is?"

Samantha nodded. "Odds are I just gave you more than you'll see this entire year from your little thespian exploits. So, note to self: it might be prudent to take another gander at exactly where your bread is buttered."

"Oh, no. Uh-uh," Eric protested. "We have a contract."

Sam folded her hands comfortably in front of herself. "Indeed. We do. One that clearly states that there are no guarantees. Humanity is fickle, Eric. It's only good business to maintain a revolving door. If another new hunk should suddenly eclipse your popularity, well—as you know—you're paid on commission."

"But you've been pushing me with the drones!" Eric blustered.

"Have been," Sam acknowledged. She let out a peeved breath and started to tap at her computer keyboard. "I'm also advertising for new faces, even as we speak. Would you care to see the size of my inbox?"

Eric struggled to maintain his footing, let alone his dignity. "Wait, so suddenly I'm on the outs here, just because I dodged some extracurricular dinner?"

Samantha held her regal head high. "I asked you to dinner to discuss the potential expansion of our business relationship at *Virtually Mine.* Even if you'd recorded this conversation, that's all you could prove."

Eric couldn't help pacing. He could hardly believe this was happening at all. "This... This isn't legal. It's not, you know, right."

If Samantha was sweating in the very least, she certainly didn't show it. Her voice remained as smooth as her scarlet silk blouse. "Eric, Sweetheart. Morality is a relative term. Actors perform intimate acts with people they don't even know, much less like, on camera for money, even awards. No matter how an agent packages it, it's still high-class harlotry. You're an actor. At least you claim to be. Let's not pretend that you have scruples."

Eric shook his head incredulously. He didn't put much stock in spiritual things, but he felt like he was dealing with the devil himself.

Waiting at Rob's door with Freddie wagging his tail at her side could have been much more enjoyable for M.J. if she hadn't been so acutely aware that she had company. Nervously, she glanced over as another Meter Mobile pulled up beside her abandoned one. M.J. whirled back as Rob opened the door.

At the sight of his master, Freddie wagged all over. Rob leaned down to pat his head. "Hey, there, Fella. Have a good time?"

M.J. smiled congenially, covering her concern the best that she could. "Yeah, he pretty much sniffed every blade of grass between here and the pier."

As Rob unhooked Freddie's leash, M.J. snuck a glance toward the street, just as the other Meter Maid got out to inspect M.J.'s abandoned vehicle. M.J. knew that this big-boned matron was every bit as humorless as she looked.

Rob nodded out toward a car out front. "That's not your car, is it? It's street sweeping day."

M.J. covered. "No, no. I walked."

Rob directed M.J.'s gaze to the two parking enforcement vehicles just down the block. "They're out in force today."

With horror, M.J. watched as the Meter Matron reached into M.J.'s vehicle and picked up M.J.'s quickly discarded uniform and man-shoes. "Yeah."

Missing her anxiety completely, Rob closed Freddie inside the house. "So, I'm curious. This business of yours—I'm surprised he gets you all to himself, that you're not walking more dogs."

M.J. sputtered. "Oh, I have lots of other...dogs. It's staggering the number of dogs I walk. Kind of a whole canine club I'm running here."

"Freddie's pretty social," Rob replied. "Might do well with the group."

Acceptingly, M.J. nodded, just as she saw the mother of all Meter Matrons take down her vehicle's license. "Speaking of which, I'd better scoot. It's a fast-paced life, this dog walking biz."

"Okay. Thanks. See you tomorrow, then." Rob stepped inside and called out to Freddie as he closed the door. "You hear that, Freddie. You're going to be in a club!"

As soon as Rob disappeared, M.J. whipped around to the street. Her heart leapt into her throat as the departing matron's Meter Mobile motored away.

What to do? At a loss for a better idea, M.J. tore across Rob's front yard in hot pursuit. In moments, M.J. skidded around the corner onto Ocean Avenue. Safely out of Rob's earshot, she cried out to the escaping vehicle. "Hey, wait... I was on my break!"

Under normal circumstances, M.J. wasn't much of a runner. But as she darted on foot past mid-day traffic, she found her inner athlete. What she'd do when she caught up with the matron, M.J. didn't really know, but she'd figure that out when it came to it.

The matron's Meter Mobile was blocks ahead, but M.J. could tell she was gaining on her. "Please, please, please...yes!" M.J. cried as the traffic light ahead turned yellow. Incredibly, the matron putted through, just as it turned red. "Stop! What are you crazy?! That was totally red!"

What she lacked in speed, M.J. made up with determination. Dissuaded only momentarily, M.J. sprinted as fast as her not so very long legs would carry her.

Why it was that Dustin and Wissy had to squarely position themselves in front of the only open exit to the theater, Kate didn't know. Everything in Kate wanted to melt into a puddle, evaporate into thin air, and quietly waft away. Despite her longing to do just that, she still found herself fighting through the clamor of ingénues lavishing praise upon Dustin, angling for the chance to be his next scene partner.

Her heart beyond flattened within her, Kate squeezed by as Wissy protectively claimed Dustin as her own, clenching him by his sculpted bicep. It was a move Dustin did nothing to discourage.

Finally free, Kate burst out of the theater and into the throng of pedestrian traffic on the popular Third Street Promenade.

A talent scout with a clipboard called out to Kate, "Hey, looking for love? I'm casting for a reality dating show."

Wordlessly, Kate blasted by him. She fought the urge to whip back with a sarcastic retort, but she pressed her lips together so nothing of what came to mind in the moment would dare exit her mouth. She knew she seemed old-fashioned, but she hated herself for even thinking the kind of things her peers didn't hesitate to say. Her mother's advice rang in her ears that what came out of a person under pressure was exactly what was bottled up inside. Sweetness or bile, the words of Kate's mouth would define her, and no matter how much her heart ached, bitter just wasn't who she was.

Instead, Kate just ran. She bolted past shoppers, street musicians, and infuriatingly cozy couples, walking hand in hand. She swerved around the corner onto Arizona Avenue where she found herself in the middle of the area's Farmer's Market. Locals ambled along, crisscrossing the street, browsing through booths for fruits and vegetables.

Weaving her way through vendors and foot traffic, Kate raced toward the bluff overlooking the Pacific, heaving with sobs. Had her eyes not been so blurred by tears, she might not have careened into M.J. who, as it happened, was barreling down the sidewalk along Ocean Avenue at the very same time, in hot pursuit of the escaping Meter Matron.

"Hey, watch where you're—" M.J. startled, realizing just who had broken her stride. "Kate! Where are you going?"

"To throw myself off that cliff," Kate blurted. "Wanna help?"

Heaving for breath, M.J. bent over. She took a forlorned last look at the escaping Meter Matron as she disappeared into the distance. M.J. stood up, offered Kate a hand, and pulled her to her feet. "Come on."

As usual, a wide assortment of actors populated the casting co-op's common area as Dustin swaggered through. Cats and their owners waited to audition. Impossibly limber ballerinas stretched and rose to their toes. Senior citizens in pajamas rehearsed. Moms went over lines with their kids.

Dustin's chest filled as he returned to Wissy's now familiar studio. It felt good to be called back, especially after the whole shirtless debacle of the first audition. What had seemed a disaster had turned into a bit of brilliance, he decided. It had not only set him apart amongst the crowd of contenders, it had also secured his spot in Wissy's good graces.

A look of dismay on her face, Wissy looked Dustin up and down as he approached, wearing the same shirt he'd just had on for their scene in class. "Where's the vest? They liked the vest. They thought you were quirky."

His bubble burst, Dustin's face fell. "Well, it wasn't mine."

"This is a callback, Dustin. I told you to wear the same thing."

"I thought you meant the same thing I wore to class."

Visibly annoyed, Wissy slapped a size card onto Dustin's palm. "What are you, bush league? You always wear the same thing you wore to the first audition. That's how they remember you. That's what got you called back."

Dustin watched, forlorned as Wissy skulked away. He distinctly noticed how quickly she softened and preened as Eric arrived. It wasn't just realizing that Eric had also been called back that ate at Dustin. It was the flirty way that Wissy sidled up to Eric, like her interests were turning Eric's way. Dustin listened intently for their exchange.

"Eric, hi," Wissy cooed.

"Hey." Eric scribbled his name on the sign-in sheet.

Wissy cozied up to Eric. "So, I heard you almost got that infomercial. Very impressive."

Eric brushed it off congenially. "Well, you know. Sometimes it comes down to a look."

Wissy leaned toward Eric and spoke in a stage whisper that Dustin couldn't help but hear. "Don't say I said so," she purred, "but it was probably about their has-been of a name star not wanting to stand next to you."

Kate and M.J. wandered along the Palisades Park path. A little air and space had gone a long way toward calming Kate's shattered spirit. It helped her get her eyes off herself to hear about what had brought M.J. to come crashing into her at exactly the right moment. The way M.J. told it, Kate couldn't help laughing. It was like someone above had known just what the two of them needed and just when they would need it, someone who orchestrated everything for the best no matter how bewildering it might seem in the short run.

Kate gave M.J.'s shoulders an encouraging squeeze as they walked along. "You should go into the office. Explain."

A smirk crossed M.J.'s lips. "Something tells me they won't go for the moonlighting as a dog walker on company time part."

"Maybe you could spin it somehow."

M.J. nodded gamely. "Oh, I could spin it. But do I really want to write parking tickets for the rest of my life anyway?"

"It's an honest living. Pays the rent."

A moment of silence passed before M.J. responded. "I guess I want more than that. Yeah, you wait tables for rent; but you've still got your acting. Some kind of dream to shoot for."

"I'm never going back to that class, again," Kate vowed. "He could have tied her shoelaces he was so far down her throat."

"Impressive in some circles."

"I mean, sure, Dustin...he's a little self-involved, but aren't they all?"

M.J. kicked at a pebble in her path. "Yeah, guys are pretty much suns and we're like these planets, orbiting around them. That's the order of the cosmos."

Kate searched her soul, sensing a palpable change. "I was pretty okay with that, but this...with her... Why do I even still want him? But I look at those eyes of his and I'm, like, sucked into his vortex again and... Blechk! I hate this! I can't believe I was starting to think he was the one. I really was." Again, hot tears filled Kate's eyes. It was over, she realized. But she wasn't over him.

"We always think the one we're seeing is the one," M.J. sympathized. "Otherwise, why bother?"

Kate threw her head back mournfully. "For three wonderful months, Dustin was practically perfect."

"Welcome to the end of the first trimester."

"Huh?"

M.J. communicated experience in the way she shook her head. "Most any guy can behave for that long, even the compulsive ones. Then, it's like—to the day—the real guy starts to pop out."

Kate wiped her tear-streaked face. "So much for my buffer boy making him jealous."

"You made me jealous," M.J. retorted. "Does that count? What with the flowers and the whole cozy-schmozy phone call."

Kate knew it was more than the flowers Brad had sent. Those were part of her rental fee. It was the way Brad seemed to go above and beyond that made Kate sigh. "I just wish Brad were real."

"Well, he is real," M.J. replied. "I mean, you talked to him. There's a real guy working your file."

The tiniest speck of hope glistened in Kate's eyes. "That's what I thought. You think so, too?"

"It wasn't a robot, was it?" M.J. adopted a mechanical cadence. "Did-he-talk-like-this?"

Kate felt herself smiling. "Not so much. It's weird. I was actually more comfortable in one conversation with him than I was the whole three months with Dustin. Too bad I only had enough on my credit card for a week. Too bad I had to buy his time at all."

M.J. threw an understanding arm around Kate. "I like to think of it as an investment. See, I'm investing in the possibilities with Rob. I'm getting out there, pushing past my comfort zone. Hey, do you happen to know where I could nab a couple of dogs?"

Walking along with her roommate, Kate felt strangely comforted. She didn't have Dustin. By the end of the rental term, she wouldn't have Brad. But side-by-side with a soon-to-be ex-Meter Maid, she knew she had the love of a friend.

Long after she knew her parents would have turned their phone ringer off, Kate thoughtfully dialed their number. Three hours ahead in Eastern Time, they retired at ten p.m. like clockwork and wouldn't pick up her call. As she waited for their outgoing message to play, she pasted Brad's flower card poem into her journal and dated it. Whoever he was, he had done his job well.

Kate's reverie was broken by a tone, signaling her to record a message. "Hey, Mom and Daddy," she started. "Sorry about the phone tag. The big news here is that Dustin and I are sort of...not so much anything anymore. It's, well...it is what it is, but I'm surviving somewhat. Haven't thought about ending it all for at least a few hours. Hyperbole, guys. No need to jump on a plane, I just...I miss you."

With that, Kate hung up the phone. She wanted what her parents had, not only a romance, but also a best friendship for life. She'd always dreamed of getting married back in Virginia at the same place where they had gotten married. She wanted to walk down the aisle of their old country church toward a guy who would adore her forever, just the way her dad treasured her mom.

Wistfully, Kate looked up at her computer screen and called up Brad's photo. She thought about the real guy he was, that guy who seemed to have gone the extra mile to help get her over the mountain of sadness she'd felt in losing Dustin. As she gazed into Brad's inviting eyes, it occurred to her that there was still time left on her rental. *What a waste*, she thought, *not to use it.*

eight

Deep in the recesses of the *Virtually Mine* stock room, Charlie sifted through floor-to-ceiling shelves of meticulously catalogued gifts, designated for the company's clientele. He passed by the stuffed animals, baubles, and candies of the introductory level and ventured beyond to the deluxe level shelves. The disparity nagged at him. Kate seemed worth so much more to him than anything the lesser levels had to offer.

Charlie picked up a white velvet jewelry box and opened the lid. Inside was a dainty gold heart on a delicate chain. He knew he couldn't jump this level for Kate, but as he admired it, he was sorely tempted. He could offer to pay for the necklace himself, he reasoned, but then again, he was sure that it would never pass muster with the company. Charlie thought of his father, whose words had a way of ringing in his ears in this sort of situation. His dad had always taught that whenever a person was tempted to do the wrong thing, even when it was for what seemed to be the right reason, a door would be thrown open to provide a way out. Charlie believed it was true. He'd seen it happen before. He just never expected that the way out of temptation would look anything at all like Samantha Raznick.

As Sam pressed through the swinging doors to the stock room, Charlie snapped the lid shut on the necklace. He quickly put it back in its place on the deluxe level shelf.

"Last time I checked, your client was still on the introductory level."

"Right. Definitely gives me an incentive to up-sell." Charlie crossed back to the introductory aisle and pulled a stuffed polar bear from the lower level shelf instead.

Charlie could feel his boss eyeing him. She was completely unnerving that way. He realized that the only thing worse than having his boss wordlessly watch him was when she actually spoke.

"Not to diminish the triumph of landing a lovely on your first day, Charlie, but one short-term client does not make you worth my while."

Charlie knew she was right. "I'm, uh, working on that. Spreading the net."

"In the mean time, I need you to assume a position," Sam continued.

Charlie's eyes bugged. "Excuse me?"

Samantha plopped a stack of client files into Charlie's spare hand. "Scan these into your system and get started with them ASAP. Archie is having his appendix out and he needs someone to take over his roster. Fake laryngitis to cover the voice change."

With that, Sam turned on her outrageously expensive heels and clicked her way out the door.

Charlie leafed through Archie's stack of clients. The fact was, for the most part, Archie's clients were an assortment of average-looking women. In a way, his heart went out to them. He knew what it was like to wear an unremarkable face. When it came down to it, he realized, every one of their clients had a forlorn spot in her heart. An Imaginary Boyfriend could help, he supposed, but deep down he knew the soul-level loneliness, that longing to be noticed for oneself that only true love could fill.

Suddenly, Charlie heard a familiar prompt from his computer. "*You've got a customer.*" Charlie looked up with a start. "I do? Oh, I do." Charlie glanced at his screen and saw an Instant Message from Kate. It read:

Brad, are you there?

Charlie's heart leapt. As he swiveled over to the computer, the entire stack of Archie's files cascaded off of his lap. He started to gather the papers, and then abandoned them for the computer.

After a moment of thought, Charlie typed out a reply IM, continuing his country boy persona as Brad: *Hey, there country girl. I've been thinkin' about you most of the day. How you doin' tonight?*

Charlie supposed he could have multi-tasked. He could have gotten a thing or two done for Archie's clients while he waited for Kate's reply, that is, if he could have torn his eyes away from the IM screen.

Finally, Kate IMed back: *Not so hot. Look, I know it's technically against the rules, but I feel like we have this amazing connection and... Is there any way I can see you?*

Charlie's hands flew up to cover his gaping mouth. What could he possibly say, even if he could work up the nerve? Reluctantly, he entered a reply: *See me? I'm really sorry, but the company has a policy about—*

Another IM from Kate popped up before Charlie could finish. It read: *I need more than a picture of a face right now. I need the person.*

Charlie took a deep breath. It was a breath so deep that he nearly hiccupped. He squeezed his eyes shut for a moment, then opened them, an idea dawning. Charlie bit his lip and tapped in a response: *Sure, Katie Mae. Can you meet me at the Ferris Wheel at nine? It's my favorite place out here.*

It wasn't long after Charlie sent that message that an inter-office memo appeared on his screen, a request from Samantha to see him in her office. Charlie tried to convince himself that it was only a coincidence, but the shake in his step as he crossed the cubicled pool persuaded him otherwise.

Though he cleared his throat to alert her that he'd reached her open door, Samantha coolly continued her work. It was as if she were intent upon making him sweat, right through his twenty-four hour deodorant.

"Did you need something?" Charlie asked.

Sam finally looked up. "It's funny," she started. "Men get exponentially more press over being visually stimulated, but the fairer sex is identically petty. Thick hair, a square jaw, broad shoulders, eyes set just the right distance apart. It all adds up to getting noticed."

Charlie wondered where Sam was going with this line of thought. He knew her well enough to assume he was approaching some sort of verbal guillotine that would drop onto his neck whether he waited silently or somehow bade her to continue. "Which means?"

Sam smiled the kind of smile that wasn't really a smile at all. "I checked your IMs. You can't see her. More to the point, she can't see you, not if you want to keep this job."

Caught, Charlie sputtered. "But she really wants to see me."

"She wants an image and a person which simply do not coincide."

Charlie's ordinary face fell.

Samantha leaned forward intently. "Trust me on this, Charlie. She wants to see the face we've sold her. She doesn't want to see you. Even if she did, she'd probably look right past you. She'll only focus on men in her basic looks class or higher. The rest are invisible."

Kate emerged from her room to find M.J. on the floor, dialing random numbers from the local phone listings.

M.J. signaled Kate for silence as she spoke into the phone. "Hi, this is M.J. Poster, Dog Walker Extraordinaire. Do you by any chance have a dog that needs walking?" M.J. put the receiver down. "Apparently not."

Kate threw a jacket over a gauzy top and jeans. "Do I look okay?"

"When do you not?"

Kate didn't usually put much thought into what she wore, but something in her worried about it this time. "I'm serious."

M.J. crossed yet another number off her call list. "So am I. Where are you going?"

"To meet him."

"Who him?"

A faint blush crossed Kate's cheeks. "My sweet little country boy."

M.J. reeled back. "Shut up!"

Kate grinned as she flung open the door. She was shocked to find Dustin standing there, just about to knock. "Dustin. Hi."

Dustin lowered his hand sheepishly. "Hey, can we talk?"

Flustered, Kate straightened her collar. "Now?"

"Believe me," Dustin pressed. "It's urgent."

Kate glanced at her watch. That thing about going with the bird in the hand over the bird in the bush came to mind, only Kate wasn't sure which guy was in which. Brad had agreed to meet her at the pier, yet there Dustin was right in front of her, pleading for her attention with those puppy dog eyes of his. As if things couldn't get any more awkward for Kate, Charlie rounded the corner into view, heading toward his apartment next door.

As Kate exchanged glances with Charlie, she couldn't help but notice disappointment flicker across his face when he saw Dustin standing at her doorway. It was easy for Kate to understand why Charlie would be disappointed in her for even thinking about letting Dustin in, especially after everything she'd confided to Charlie when he'd come to fix her sink. She wanted to be strong enough to resist Dustin's charms, but then again, he had claimed an urgent reason for being there. Maybe this timing wasn't as awkward as it seemed, she reasoned. Maybe it was meant to be.

Dustin plopped onto Kate's bed and leaned back against her headboard. "I completely tanked. My first callback for a national and I fully reeked."

Kate stood just inside the door. A glance at her nightstand confirmed the clock's advance toward the time she had set up with Brad. "Maybe it wasn't that bad."

Dustin grabbed a piece of candy from Kate's dish and popped it into his mouth. "They liked me quirky from the first call where I was wearing this floofy kind of vest I bummed off some granny, which of course I didn't have today. So, I had to do something to set myself apart and I thought—I know, a twitch." Dustin's eyes lit up as he reenacted his own ingenuity. "Yeah, a twitch could not only be quirky, get it? It's also a possible side effect of their medicine."

Kate couldn't help marveling to herself that, apparently, this was Dustin's definition of urgent. "So, what did they say?"

"Thank you," Dustin spat. "Don't you hate that?"

"Back home 'thank you' means they appreciate you."

Dustin shook his head. "Yeah, well, it's the kiss of death here. Wissy barely spoke to me. She said she's going to call you, though."

There was something almost amazing to Kate that anything about this conversation had to do with her. "Wissy is calling me? Why?"

Dustin rolled his eyes. "Some other commercial they're casting Monday. She said you're perfect. But trust me on this: whatever she says about wardrobe, still wear a shirt."

Kate nodded, covering how oddly this struck her, let alone how surreal this entire conversation was beginning to feel. "Dustin, why did you come over?"

Dustin crumpled his candy wrapper into a little ball and put it on Kate's desk. "I needed to talk to you. You wouldn't believe how bad my day was."

Kate reeled, struggling to fathom what she'd ever seen in Dustin.

"She'll never call me in again," he pouted.

Kate cocked her head quizzically. "Oh, I don't know. She seemed fairly into you in class."

"That was acting," he corrected. "Remember?"

Exasperated, Kate headed for the door. "Dustin, I've gotta go."

Dustin sat up, a look of shock on his face. "What, you're kicking me out? I'm having a crisis here."

"Which you can feel free to have without me." Kate offered. "Stay, go, do what you have to do. I've just gotta... Bye." With that, Kate bolted out the door.

As Kate flew down the apartment building's stairs, she kicked herself for having stayed at all. *How long would Brad wait for her?* She could only pray that she wasn't too late.

Charlie was near the foot of the apartment stairs, refilling the swimming pool with a hose. "Kate, hi. Where're you going?"

Kate picked up speed. "Where I should have gone half an hour ago."

Kate blasted by. Charlie whipped around with the hose, dousing the walk with water. As Kate quickly sidestepped the flood, Charlie dropped the hose, which, taking on a life of its own, curled up and thrashed about, spraying water everywhere.

"Sorry!" Charlie called after her as she disappeared into the garage.

As cute as Kate's ragtop was, the old car could be temperamental. This night, of all nights, it was downright testy. Hurriedly, she ground at the ignition, but the thing flatly refused to turn over. "*Come on...*" Nothing.

Quickly, Kate regrouped. The pier was only a mile away, ten minutes if she made a run for it. Not wanting to waste another moment, she abandoned her car and raced down the walk. The sun had long since set and the bright lights of the Ferris Wheel beckoned her. "*I'm coming, Brad! Please stay...*"

By the time Kate arrived at the bridge to the pier, she was breathing hard and not just a little bit dewy. All she could do was hope that Brad would understand. Kate pressed through the meandering crowd, searching for Brad's now familiar face, as she hastened toward the Ferris Wheel. "*Please still be here...*" Kate hated herself for being late. It wasn't that she blamed Dustin for coming over as much as she blamed herself for giving into him. She resolved that it would be the last time.

Finally, Kate skidded to a stop at the ticket gate below the Ferris Wheel. She scanned the nearby crowd, searching desperately. "Brad! Brad..." Not seeing him, Kate slumped in defeat. *How long had he waited for her?* Surely, she'd missed him. Sadly, Kate turned to go

Suddenly, the ride's attendant called out to her. "Hey, are you Kate Valentine?"

Kate's eyes brightened with hope. "Yeah, yeah. That's me. I'm Kate Valentine."

"Some guy told me to give these to you." With that the attendant handed Kate a ticket for the ride and a fluffy white polar bear with a *VM* heart logo on its chest.

Kate glanced around. "Did he leave...the guy who gave you this?"

The attendant nodded. "He said to tell you he had to go, but he hopes you have a good time." With that, the attendant opened the gate to the ride.

There was something dreamlike to Kate about accepting Brad's gifts and walking through the gate. It felt as if there were much more to the steps she was taking than met the natural eye. Though she walked through and boarded a Ferris Wheel car all by herself, somehow she sensed that she was far from alone.

As the attendant started the ride, Kate seated the polar bear beside her and lowered the security bar. Then, just as the Ferris Wheel began to turn, Kate's cell phone rang. *Private Caller* flashed on her screen.

Charlie pulled the brim of his cap low as he waited for Kate to answer her phone. He watched, a safe distance away, obscured from her by the throng. He had set it all up with the attendant on his way home. He'd raced back over to be with Kate, unnoticed.

"Hello?" Kate answered.

Charlie couldn't help but melt at the sound of her voice. It had a musical lilt to it, just like his mom's used to have.

Taking on Brad's persona, Charlie answered. "Hey, there Katie-girl. I'm so glad you came." Charlie watched as Kate glanced around below, confident that with hundreds of people milling around the pier, she'd never pick him out.

"Brad, where are you?"

Below, Charlie hung back as he watched Kate's ascent on the Ferris Wheel. "Closer than you think, Darlin'. I'm afraid my boss was monitoring my IMs with you this afternoon. She said if I met you in person, she'd have to let me go."

"Oh, no."

Encouraged by Kate's sympathetic tone, Charlie continued as Brad. "That's why I brought Bubba along to keep you company. I warned him not to get fresh." Charlie saw Kate as she looked over at the polar bear, charmed.

"So far, he's behaving himself very well," she replied.

Charlie breathed a bit easier. It was working. "Anyhow, I figured this way we could at least be together without me breaking any promises. Much as I want to be right there beside you, I have a thing about bein' true to my word."

"And you're really right here?" Kate asked. She leaned over to look below.

"Not a stone's skip away. Close enough to see how cute you look with your hair blowin' in your eyes like that."

Kate brushed her hair behind her ear. "Thanks for staying. Sorry I was so late."

"Don't you worry 'bout that a second, Girl. You are so worth the wait." Charlie craned to see as

Kate's car crested the top of the Wheel, giving her a breathtaking view of the city lights. It thrilled him to see her there.

"I always liked Ferris Wheels," Kate replied. "But it's been forever, since the county fair back home. All these months here and I'd never ridden this one."

"Life just seems simpler up there, doesn't it? Lookin' down on all those twinklin' lights..."

"Yeah," Kate agreed.

"I used to ride one whenever I'd had a hard day. And I thought it might put a smile back on that pretty little face of yours." As Kate's car started its descent, Charlie saw the smile that curled on Kate's lips. "There it is."

Kate quickly covered her face, clearly delighted. "You saw that?"

"I did," Charlie answered. "Hey, you want some kettle corn?" He watched as Kate's mouth dropped open.

"How did you know? It's, like, my biggest weakness."

Charlie glanced back down the pier as he spoke into the phone. "Well, go on over to the stand when you get off 'cause I got you some waitin'. Don't forget Bubba, now."

"Oh, I won't."

When Charlie saw Kate put an affectionate arm around Bubba, he just about passed out on the spot.

The fact that things were going so well helped Charlie to work up his nerve. As himself he'd always been so skittish around Kate, but as Brad he was finally able to say what had been on his heart since the first time he'd laid eyes on her. "Speakin' of weaknesses, you know what my biggest weakness is gettin' to be?"

Kate adjusted the phone at her ear. "What?"

Charlie smiled softly, gazing across the crowd to the loveliest girl he knew. "My biggest weakness... It's you, Katie Mae Valentine. It's gettin' to be you."

nine

Every once in a while, M.J. happened upon what could only be described as a stroke of genius, at least by her own personal assessment. It was Saturday, which meant that the local animal advocates would have any number of potential pets penned outside to show off to passing pedestrians in the popular shopping district.

It wasn't that M.J. frequented the doggie rescue mission she'd seen set up on the corner every weekend. What with her allergies, if anything she'd steered clear of it. But it was situated right across the way from her favorite yogurt shop, and something about the combination of non-fat Mango Splash and seeing all those dogs frolicking behind temporary fences gave her an idea.

M.J. spooned the fruity confection into her mouth as she scanned a diverse lot of pups. The assortment was worlds apart from the purebreds and show dogs of the doggie day care place the Westside elite frequented, the one where she'd written scores of double-parking tickets, as the rich dropped off their perfectly groomed pets to be pampered.

With a blast from her inhaler, M.J. ventured closer to the pet adoption cages. It wasn't that these dogs weren't cute in their own way, but the mix of mutts and older breeds did look sorely in need of rescue.

For a little while, M.J. watched as passersby gravitated to the best looking dogs in the lot. That was the way it always went, M.J. thought. Feeling somewhere between a mutt and a runt herself, M.J. sympathized. She'd lost count of the number of times she'd been overlooked in favor of prettier girls. So, there was something in her that understood why the homelier pups wagged their tails so eagerly and ate up any affection they got all the more.

A volunteer approached M.J. "The Dalmatians make wonderful pets if you're looking for a bigger dog, but I just adore the little Sheltie mix. Don't you want to just eat her up?"

"Actually, I had breakfast," M.J. cracked. "How much are they?"

"They're free to a good home." The woman scooped up the Sheltie mix before M.J. could stop her. "Shortie, here, will need to be fixed soon."

M.J. examined Shortie skeptically. "Fixed? Something wrong with him?"

The volunteer looked M.J. over with a more than condescending smile. "You've never owned a dog, have you?"

Locals trolled a yard sale just in front of Charlie's building. When Kate had knocked on Charlie's door to ask for a hand setting it up, he'd been all too happy to assist. He'd gone beyond simply carting her excess housewares, electronics, and knickknacks down to the walk. He'd also stuck around to help arrange things attractively for display.

What Kate needed yard sale money for, Charlie didn't know for sure, so he kept his ears peeled as he spread out her items for sale. When Kate had mentioned to him that her car was on the blink, he'd volunteered to take a look at it to save her from having it towed. For the mean time, he'd loaned her his motorized razor scooter to help her get around. It felt so good to take care of her, in every way that he could.

Charlie winced with concern when he saw that Mrs. Teasdale had ventured out of her apartment to inspect Kate's brocade Victorian chair. For starters, he knew Mrs. Teasdale was a bit of a packrat, and he couldn't imagine where she'd even find room for it. He was also pretty sure that it wouldn't be a week before one or the other of her cats would claw the upholstery to shreds.

"I don't know," Mrs. Teasdale picked. "It's got this little scratch on the leg."

Clearly wanting to make the sale, Kate returned a winning smile. "That's from where I nicked it with my ice-skates when I was seven. Every imperfection tells a story. They give it more character. Truth is, I kind of hate to give it up."

"Fifteen dollars," Mrs. Teasdale quibbled.

Kate pursed her lips congenially, considering the offer. "I know it's worth a hundred. I need at least forty."

"Twenty or I'll live with what I've got."

Kate shot a weakening glance over to Charlie. He could see her buckling under the pressure. Quickly, Charlie pulled some bills out of his wallet. "Kate, just a... I'll give you fifty."

Mrs. Teasdale whirled about. "Charlie! You know very well I spoke for it first."

Kate turned appreciatively to Charlie. "Really?"

Charlie nodded as calmly as his pounding heart would allow. "You can come over and sit on it any time you want, Mrs. Teasdale. But you have a lot of chairs and I could really use this one. For sitting."

"Charlie, you're an angel!" Just like that, Kate threw her arms around Charlie and gave him a spontaneous hug.

There were two things that Charlie realized immediately. One: it was the first time he'd ever been embraced by a woman within three decades of his age. (He didn't factor in his mom, his cousins, or any of his dad's older parishioners.) And Two: Kate's hair smelled of tangerines, which he immediately decided was his favorite fruit.

Charlie could feel his face going scarlet. He worried that Kate might notice until he saw that her attention had been diverted over his shoulder to M.J., who was fast approaching with two small dogs on leashes.

M.J. froze, agape at the sight of Kate's yard sale. "Kate! That...wait, that's your microwave! Remind me never to leave you unsupervised on Saturdays. What are you doing?!"

Kate returned a cheery grin. "Selling my stuff. Wanna buy it?"

"It's already ours," M.J. insisted as Shortie, the Sheltie mix, and a yet to be named part Chihuahua yipped at a passing poodle. "What are we supposed to cook with? Shortie, no!"

"We can use the stovetop. The oven. It'll be fun, just like in the olden days. I need the money." Kate stooped down to give the pups on M.J.'s leashes some attention. "Where did you get these dogs?"

"Adopted, like me." M.J. turned to Charlie. "Charlie, I know, I know. I'll give you a deposit."

Before Charlie had a chance to respond, M.J. rotated around to Kate. "Back up. You're selling off life and limb for what?"

Even though Kate lowered her voice to sotto tones, Charlie was still close enough to overhear. "For him," Kate said.

M.J.'s brow furrowed. "Who him?"

Charlie leaned closer, as discreetly as he could, his curiosity piqued.

"Him-him," Kate whispered. "You know."

M.J. rocked back, her volume increasing. "You mean, your imaginary rent-a-guy?"

Kate snapped a finger to her lips. "Shhh! And he's not imaginary. He's real. You said it yourself."

"I meant real in the sense that he's human as opposed to actually being your boyfriend."

Charlie listened in, hardly believing his ears as Kate went on, her face growing more animated.

"It hit me this morning like, bing!" Kate enthused. "The week I had with him is almost over. I can't let that happen. Sure my credit card is maxed now, and I have to reserve rent, but I don't need all this stuff and it's as good as gold."

"Aren't you still paying for half of this on that credit card?" M.J. protested. "Isn't that sort of why it's maxed?"

Kate glanced around at her former purchases. "All the better to pay it off. What do I need with a wok, or a foot massager, or a DVD player—"

"You're selling the DVD player?!"

"Why keep it when I sold the TV?"

"Noooo!" M.J. roared.

Kate hiked her eyebrows with glee. "I got seventy-five bucks for it. Can you believe it?"

M. J. buckled at the knees. "Kate, this is crazy."

"I know it seems nuts, but Mom always said, love makes you do kooky things."

Charlie steadied himself against the back of his newly purchased chair. It kept him from keeling straight over.

"Love?" M.J. spouted. "Who said anything about love?"

Kate smiled understandingly. "Maybe it sounds ridiculous but—"

"That's because it is!" M.J. spat.

In a way, Charlie was glad that M.J. continued the conversation, but the turn it was taking worried him.

Kate didn't miss a beat. "You're the one who was all about investing in the possibilities."

"I said 'invest' not divest!"

A dreamy look crossed Kate's face as she leaned toward M.J. confidentially. "You know what he told me last night? That I'm his first girlfriend ever."

M.J. shook her head. "And you believed him? A guy who looks like that? He's playing you. And all his other clients. He probably read it off a script."

"No. Uh-uh," Kate answered. "I get a really genuine kind of vibe from him."

M.J. yanked at her already unruly hair. "This is madness. I am living with a loony bag."

"I'm a loony bag?" Kate retorted. "Am I the one who's allergic to dogs and just adopted two of them?"

Just then, a woman pushed past Charlie toward Kate. "Hey, how low can you go for the treadmill?"

Kate turned receptively. "One-fifty, firm."

M.J. positioned herself between them. "Stop it, Kate! No."

Immediately, the woman shook Kate's hand. "Done."

"Kate, this is insanity!" M.J. implored.

Kate took her roommate by the shoulders. She looked her square in the face. "It's just stuff, M.J., really. I don't need it, any of it. Look, all I know is, I don't want to wake up one day, sorry for what might have been. I have a feeling about this guy. I do. And I've just got to go for it."

Kate zipped through traffic on Charlie's motorized razor scooter. She glided to a stop in front of the casting co-op, picked up the scooter, and raced inside.

There was only a minute or two for Kate to find the right studio, sign in, and speed through her lines. Soon, she heard Wissy call out above the din of the busy waiting area.

"Okay, Kate and Jerry, you're up." As Kate and Jerry rose, Wissy called out again. "Anybody else, come in with them for the explanation."

Kate followed Jerry into the casting studio, the scooter in tow. A director and an ad exec barely looked up as a half a dozen other actors squeezed into the room. Scanning the other auditionees, Kate did a double take at the last guy in line.

It was Brad.

Kate caught her breath. It couldn't be, but it was. There was no mistaking Brad's face from the photo that she'd been sent from *Virtually Mine*. Suddenly, Kate realized, her Imaginary Boyfriend wasn't so imaginary. Everything in Kate tingled. Her stomach flip-flopped.

Wissy stepped in front of the auditionees. "Everybody listening. This is casting very quickly, so be reachable. You're at a party. Very casual. Guys approach, turn on the charm. Ladies, you like him a lot, so do your best to keep up appearances, even when you sense your obviously inferior hygiene product is, shall we say, letting you down."

Try as she might, Kate could not keep her eyes off Brad. She attempted not to be too obvious, but couldn't help cutting her eyes to him. At least he was so focused on Wissy that he didn't catch her.

Wissy waltzed toward the door. "Okay, Kate and Jerry stay. Everybody else out. Size cards and photos on the table."

Kate watched as Brad exited. He had been the last in the door, so he also was the first out. Everything in Kate hoped to get Brad's attention, but she was first up and the session was ready to start.

Wissy stepped behind the camera to shoot. "Kate, you can put your scooter down there."

Kate shyly stepped to the side and propped the scooter against the wall, dying to follow Brad, but knowing she couldn't, at least not yet. She reminded herself that he'd still be there when she finished, waiting for his turn to audition.

Wissy pointed to two small pieces of white tape on the carpet. "So, on the marks. Give us your names, then go right into it."

First in line, Jerry started. "Hi, I'm Jerry Fontaine."

Wissy panned to Kate. "And you're..."

Distracted, Kate turned back to the camera. "Uh...Kate Valentine." Kate fought to rally her focus, hoping somehow that her discombobulation would play in to the scene.

Jerry began, in character. He barely refered to his lines. "Hi...you know, I couldn't help but notice you. That white dress...you look so amazing in it."

A demure smile crossed Kate's face. "Thanks."

Jerry extended his hand to her. "I'm Michael."

"Michael. I'm... Listen, I'm really sorry. But could you excuse me?" With that, Kate walked away, grabbed Charlie's scooter and headed straight for the studio door.

Wissy stopped recording. "Okay, good. Kate that was just what we were going for—"

Barely acknowledging Wissy, the director, or the ad exec, Kate opened the door to leave. "Great. Thanks."

Kate knew it was customary to wait to be excused, but something inside her had shifted. Suddenly, she didn't care about living in the imaginary world of acting, not when the real, live version of Brad was waiting outside. Just before she pulled the door closed, she heard Jerry's bemused voice say, "So, I guess that's it?"

Kate scanned the busy waiting area for Brad's familiar face. Finally, she spotted him. There he was, across the room, working with his audition partner.

Her heart pounding furiously, Kate approached, listening in on their rehearsal of the commercial's copy.

"I'm Michael," he said.

"Michael. I'm... Listen, I'm really sorry, but could you excuse me?"

As Brad's partner wandered off in character, Kate gathered her courage. She stepped up behind him and called out, "Brad?"

Right away, he turned back to Kate and flashed a receptive smile. "Hi. Actually, it's Eric."

Kate returned an understanding grin. "No, really. You're working under a stage name here, right?"

Eric showed her his headshot. He pointed to where his name, Eric Bender, was printed at the bottom. "No, it's really Eric. See?"

Confused, Kate pulled Brad's snapshot out of her pocket. "No, it's... Look, you're even wearing the same jacket."

In a moment, Eric recognized the shot and nodded with realization.

Kate took a step closer, checking around to make sure she wasn't overheard. "Brad, it's okay. You didn't break any promises. Us running into each other, it was totally an accident. How can your boss fire you over that?"

Eric rubbed at his clean-shaven jaw good-naturedly. "Actually, she's not my boss anymore. I'm picking up my last check right after this. And this is kind of awkward...but my name, it isn't really Brad."

A light started to dawn for Kate. "Oh. Okay, Eric, gotcha. Of course. They had you use another name...but I'm used to hearing you with your accent. Without it, I didn't even recognize your voice."

All too soon for Kate, Wissy called out from the studio door. "Judy, Eric! You're up!"

Though Judy headed over immediately, Eric lingered. He softened to an understanding tone as he spoke to Kate. "Look, I'm really sorry, but it's just...I'm not that guy. I was only a face they hired for one of their Operators to hide behind. Truth is, I'm an actor, just like you, reduced to reading for embarrassments like this so I can eat."

Wissy's voice rang out again. "Eric, let's go."

Overwhelmed and humiliated, Kate fought tears. She could see Eric floundering about what to do. "It's all right," she assured. "I should have known."

"I feel really bad that... Are you going to be okay?"

Understanding, Kate pulled herself together. "Go. Get the job. I'm fine."

A reluctant look on his face, Eric left.

Tears spilling down her cheeks, Kate watched Eric go. She tracked with him all the way across the waiting area till he followed Wissy into the studio and closed the door.

For a while, Kate just stood there in shock, her face streaked. He had seemed beyond perfect for her, too perfect, she realized. What it was that had made her fall so hard so fast, Kate didn't know. All she knew was that her heart was breaking all over again, on a level far beyond the healing properties of full-fat Rocky road.

As fast as her feet would carry her, Kate fled from the casting studios, outside where she could be alone with the complete and utter fool she felt sure she'd just made of herself.

Across town, Charlie sat quietly at his *Virtually Mine* Operator's station, staring at Kate's picture. He recalled what she'd said about love. *Could it be?* Inspired, he picked up his desk phone and dialed, once again adopting Brad's country boy twang.

Charlie listened to Kate's outgoing message, enjoying the cadence of her voice. He knew she wasn't there and how much she enjoyed coming home to find the light blinking on her answering machine. Via the disguise of a phone call, he would give her what she'd bargained for and more. He would pour out every unapologetically affectionate thought that crossed his ever-loving mind.

"Hey, Katie-girl," he started. "Sorry I missed you, but I was just thinkin' of you...which for me has become a constant state of affairs these days. I know this whole imaginary thing is, well, it is what it is, but somehow... It's just that my real heart's got itself wrapped so far around you I'm not sure what to do."

It was easy for Charlie to get lost in talking to Kate, so easy that he almost didn't notice that Samantha had slipped up behind him. Only the scent of her perfume gave her presence away.

Charlie glanced back. He caught Samantha's eye, then quickly turned back to the phone. "I, uh...I gotta go for now, Katie, but listen for me. I'll be callin' again soon."

Charlie put the receiver back on its cradle and turned to Samantha sheepishly.

Sam studied him. "You are quite good. I've obviously underestimated you. Close my eyes and I'd have been charmed myself."

Charlie wasn't sure whether or not to take this as praise. "Really?"

"No wonder that she re-upped this morning, bumped to the deluxe level to boot."

Stunned, Charlie rose. "She did?"

Sam's complimentary tone took on a decided chill. "Which would have pleased me no end had I not received three complaints from Archie's clients who haven't heard a peep from you. Explanation?"

Charlie grappled with what to say. Indeed, he'd spent a fair amount of time looking over Archie's files. He'd sent out some cards, emails, and gifts. It's just that he hadn't exactly serviced them with phone calls yet. "I've been, uh...developing a plan," he explained, "a strategy, you know...catered specifically to the profiles of—"

"Make the calls." Samantha steamed away.

Turning back to his desk, Charlie reached for Archie's stack of files. He flipped the first one open, then skipped to the second, wondering how on God's green earth he could muster up interest in calling anyone other than Kate.

As Wissy trained her camera on Eric's audition with Judy, Eric could tell it was going well, at least for him. Judy was nothing to jump up and down about, but there was no mistaking that Wissy was firmly in his corner.

Judy referred to her script. "Michael. I'm... Listen, I'm really sorry, but could you excuse me?"

As Judy walked away, Wissy stepped from behind the lens. "Judy, thanks. Eric, could you hang outside for me?"

"Sure." There it was, Eric exuded. Just as he'd thought. As he waited outside the door, Eric's confidence rose.

Soon, Wissy emerged, leaning close so as not to be overheard. "Eric, that was excellent."

"Did you want me to stay and read with someone else?"

Wissy checked around secretively. "Actually, it's all very hush-hush, but this casting director I'm working for, I'm thinking you could be right for a film she's just starting."

Impressed, Eric took the bait. "Really?"

Wissy smiled coyly and extended her card. "Here's my number. The script is under lock and key, but if you wanted to swing by my apartment

Saturday night and read over my shoulder, let's just say that I wouldn't stop you." With an inviting look, Wissy went back into the casting studio and closed the door behind herself.

Eric gazed at Wissy's card, and then pitched it into the trash. She was another Samantha Raznick in the making. This time he would dodge that bullet. As he stopped to sign out, he noticed Kate's picture and info card lying on the studio's table. *She was really pretty. Sweet, too*, he remembered. Quickly, he grabbed a pencil and jotted down Kate's number and address.

Still outside the casting studios, Kate keyed a password into her cell to check her machine at home. An incredulous look crossed her face as she retrieved a message from Brad, at least whoever the real guy was, the one operating under Eric's facade. She listened as her Imaginary spoke:

"*I know this whole imaginary thing is—well, it is what it is—but somehow...it's just that my real heart's got itself wrapped so far around you I'm not sure what to do.*"

Even knowing he couldn't hear her, Kate talked to her machine. "You're not Eric. Who are you?"

The message continued. "*I, uh...I gotta go for now, Katie, but listen for me. I'll be callin' again soon.*"

A beep signaled the end of the message. Kate saved the message, and then put the phone away, her resolve building. "Not if I get to you first."

Kate's timing wasn't always perfect, but as providence would have it on this particular day, it was nigh on impeccable. Kate checked around the corner just in time to see Eric as he exited the casting studios. She dropped behind a bushy hibiscus, watching as he got into his car.

Kate looked at Charlie's scooter helplessly and scanned the nearby street. There was no way she could keep up. Frustratingly, the only cab around wasn't in service. A portly cabbie sat in the front, downing a submarine sandwich. Kate jumped into the back seat, as much to hide from Eric's departing car as to commandeer the cab.

His mouth half full, the cabbie shook his head. "No can do. I'm carbo-loading."

"There's a fat tip in it for you." Kate reached for her wallet.

At that, the cabbie put his lunch aside and started his engine. "I do hear Atkins is good."

Kate tracked Eric's car intently as it motored down the street. "Just don't lose that guy."

ten

When it came to sneezes, there were two types of women. There were demure sneezers like Kate, whose daintily pitched ka-choos bordered on amusing. Then, there were the window-rattling explosions that erupted out of M.J., no matter how hard she tried to stifle them. Alone in her apartment except for the two dogs jumping excitedly at her feet, M.J. sneezed to high heaven.

M.J. reached into her closet for a jacket. "Alright, already. I'm coming. But could I please just put on a—" Another sneeze reverberated through the apartment. Neither Shortie nor ChaCha (the name M.J. had taken to calling the scrawny part Chihuahua) seemed to notice at all as she scratched at her spreading case of hives. "I'm fine, Guys. No problem. Just reminds me to dose." With that M.J. downed a couple of allergy caps.

By the time Freddie had joined M.J.'s dog walking brigade, M.J. was feeling better. Whether it was the meds kicking in or the open air of the park, she didn't know. But with Freddie, Shortie, and ChaCha prancing along on their leashes ahead of her, M.J.'s assurance grew. She was multitasking, she thought. She was legit. She was walking three dogs, getting some exercise, and talking to Kate on her cell, all at the same time.

"I'm following him," she heard Kate exude.

M.J. adjusted the phone at her ear. "What do you mean, you're following him? I thought you said he's not the guy."

"Yes, but he said he's going to the *Virtually Mine* headquarters and their address is unlisted."

"Possibly for this very reason."

"I'm just going to see where it's located," Kate explained. "The real guy behind the model works there."

Catching sight of a nearby squirrel, Freddie began to bark.

"I think I heard stalking was upgraded to felony status in California," M.J. quipped.

"What, are you worried that Rob's going to turn you in?"

Suddenly, Freddie, Shortie, and ChaCha were all straining at their leashes, anxious to get at the squirrel. M.J. did her best to control them. "Hey, I'm working for the guy. That's different."

"So, maybe I'll apply for a job at *Virtually Mine*," Kate answered.

Freddie led the charge as M.J.'s canine club yanked free of her grasp. Abruptly, M.J. pocketed her cell and gave chase to the scattering dogs, their red nylon leashes trailing behind them. "Freddie, come back! Shortie, ChaCha, no!"

Though Freddie remained intent upon the squirrel, Shortie and ChaCha high-tailed it in two different directions. With no time to make a decision, M.J. ran after Freddie, who leapt right over a picnic table where two old gents were playing checkers, scattering their game-pieces everywhere.

"Sorry!" M.J. bolted onward, crashing into a jogger.

"Watch it!" the jogger groused.

"Freddie, wait!" M.J. cried.

Finally, the squirrel that had started the whole melee skittered up a tree in the center of a garden. Freddie attempted to follow, leaping at the tree trunk, barking repeatedly at his fluffy-tailed prey.

Seeing her chance, M.J. followed Freddie into the flowerbed and dove onto the bare dirt to snatch his leash. Filthy, she rose and held the leash up, shouting victoriously. "There! Got ya! I am still M.J. Poster, Dog Walker Extraordinaire!"

As if on cue, the sprinkler system started with a vengeance, dousing M.J. and Freddie completely.

Still riding in the cab, Kate listened closely to M.J.'s abandoned phone line. "M.J.? Where'd you go?"

The cabbie glanced back at Kate in his rear-view mirror. "He's parking. You want out here?"

"Oh! Yeah. Thanks."

With that, the cabbie pulled over to the curb.

Kate paid the driver the fat tip she'd promised and exited the cab, scooter in hand. She ducked out of sight as Eric fed his parking meter just up the block, then watched as he entered a swanky high-rise office building.

This was it, she realized. These were the offices of *Virtually Mine.*

Stealthily, Kate peered through the tinted front windows, tracking Eric as he boarded an elevator. As soon as the door glided shut, Kate entered the lobby, carrying the scooter. She studied the passing floors' lights above the elevator as they illuminated, marking Eric's upward progress.

The security guard at the desk broke Kate's concentration. "Is there something I can help you with, Miss?"

Kate wasn't one to lie, even to fib very often, but given the back-against-the-wall circumstances, she rationalized tweaking the truth to her advantage. She would treat this situation as an improvisational exercise, like Antonio had often suggested in acting class. He had said that they should practice in real life, and Kate decided to do just that.

Reaching back to her Virginia roots, Kate turned on her Southern charm as she twisted toward the guard. "Me...uh, yes, I hope so. I'm here from Virginia, and it's my boyfriend's last day on his job. I thought I'd drop by to cheer him up, but shhhhh! 'Cause it's a big surprise an' all. He works in this buildin' at a place called Virtually Mine. You know where that is, Sweet Pea?"

The guard pointed Kate toward the building's directory. "Nothing here by that name."

Kate quickly scanned the board. There it was: *V.M. Enterprises*, with Samantha Raznick's name and the suite number listed right beside it.

Kate spun back to the guard winningly. "That's it. *V.M. Enterprises*, third floor. And me, I'm so completely goofy that I went and called it by the wrong name."

The security guard eyed Kate, clearly softening. "I'm not really supposed to let anyone I don't know onto that elevator without checking ahead."

Kate eased toward the stairway. "Believe me, I understand completely. Rules are rules. I'll go run up these stairs instead and thank you for the exercise. Just remember..." With a playful flick of the wrist, Kate locked her lips, and then glided through the stairwell door. She tucked the scooter into her tote and headed up the stairs.

As unobtrusively as she could, Kate padded through the daunting double doors and into the plushly appointed lobby of *Virtually Mine*. A name placard announced that stylishly dressed Levon Mink was the guy perched at the reception desk filing his nails. Levon cut his eyes only briefly to observe Kate's arrival.

It was hard not to feel conspicuous in this place. For one thing, Kate realized that she was the only person in the room wearing a dress. The rest of the lobby was populated by an assortment of hunky guys, either leafing through magazines or checking their smart phones. *Job applicants*, Kate supposed.

With things growing more awkward by the second, Kate drew a deep breath and gamely approached Levon. "I'm here to see Samantha Raznick."

Levon raised his eyes dubiously at Kate. Other than his lids, he barely moved. "No, you're not."

Though she could tell her wiles weren't cutting it with him, Kate smiled. "It's about the job."

Levon resumed his nail filing. "Wrong again, Doll Face. She doesn't do girls."

"Excuse me?

"She hires guys. Exclusively."

Kate pondered it for a moment, and then leaned into the desk confidentially. "Perhaps I should have introduced myself. My name is Katherine Mae, and I take it that Ms. Raznick has heard of the Equal Employment Opportunity Commission."

Only too glad to be finished with his shift, Dustin removed his apron. His hopes of saying goodbye to the Doo-Wop Dinette had pretty much gone into the dumper after his whole no-vest callback debacle. He was also fairly sure that Wissy had moved onto passing her casting favors to Eric.

What Eric had that he didn't was beyond Dustin's grasp. All he knew was that he didn't like the guy any more than the turn his life seemed to be taking. Clearly, something had fizzled for him with Kate, though he couldn't imagine what on earth it was.

Dustin studied Reesa as she rang up an order for one of their regulars. As soon as the truck driver ambled out, Dustin sidled right up to Reesa. They exchanged an awkward glance or two before Dustin took it as his cue to speak. "Reesa, you're a woman."

Reesa closed the register drawer. "You had a fifty-fifty chance of getting that one right."

Dustin lowered his voice. "Well, I was thinking about getting back with Kate."

An amused grin curled on Reesa's lips. "Casting babe shined you on, did she?"

Dustin nodded. "And trust me, I've learned my lesson."

Reesa put her hands on her substantial hips. "And tell me, what is that? That lesson you learned."

Dustin drummed his fingers on his cheek, completely stumped. He thought about it long and hard, then shrugged his shoulders. "Whatever. I just learned it. And I want to get back with Kate. I've thought about it a lot, and I think it would be best for me."

Reesa shook her head. "For you."

"And Kate, too. Obviously."

Reesa leaned back against the counter. "So, just what did you have in mind to do? To get her back."

What to do, Dustin thought. What he needed was a plan, a sure-fire strategy. His face lit up as an idea struck. "Well, she seems to want me to know stuff about her. You wouldn't by any chance know anything about her, would you?"

Rob Galloway opened his front door. There stood a muddy, drenched M.J. with a sheepish smirk on her face.

Rob looked for the other dogs as he let Freddie inside. "Wow. Where's the rest of the pack?"

M.J. glanced back toward the park sheepishly. "Kind of on a spontaneous field trip. Freddie wasn't so much on going, what with the bus ride and the name tags and... You totally know I'm lying, right?"

"I do." In a way, it was a relief to Rob that M.J. fessed up. It saved him the trouble of calling her bluff. "Sussing out the real deal kind of goes with the therapist territory."

M.J. shuffled uneasily. "Yeah. Okay, here's the thing. I just returned the other dogs to the place where I got them because...I'm not a dog walker."

"You aren't."

"And there's a fairly good chance that this is the extra meds talking and that I won't remember much of this tomorrow, but I'm a Meter Maid. At least I was, till I saw you in the park and thought this might be a good way to meet you."

Rob couldn't help back-peddling a bit. "You invented a business with cards and dogs and—"

"Got fired from my job, don't forget that," M.J. added.

Rob looked at M.J. amazed. "You got fired?"

"I did," M.J. nodded. "And what, you might ask, is the point anyway? I mean, A) You're adorable. B) You're completely out of my league, then C) I'm so freakishly allergic to your dog that I'm at risk of becoming a rampant over-the-counter drug addict, and D)—"

"—and D)," Rob interjected, "I don't own Freddie. I'm just taking care of him this month for a friend."

Rob watched as M.J. rocked back in shock for a moment, and then started to edge away insecurely. "No, no. Erase, erase, erase. Freddie's yours."

Rob shook his head. "Uh-uh."

A desperate look came over M.J.'s face. "He has to be. That way you can close that door and I can go pine about how our sweet, sad parting was totally about the dog and not about you rejecting me."

"M.J..."

M.J. raised a hand to stop him. "There's a fine line between tragic and pathetic, Rob. And I'm begging you, please. Let me stay on this side of it."

An assortment of *Virtually Mine* presents in his arms, Charlie stopped to look at the white velvet box one more time. There was the little gold heart necklace he could finally give to Kate, now that she'd signed up for the deluxe level. Affectionately, Charlie closed the velvet box and put it atop the stack of gifts he'd gathered.

What Charlie wouldn't give for Kate, he thought. She was like that pearl of great price his dad always used to teach about from the pulpit. Charlie wasn't sure that his father would have completely approved of the way he was going about things with Kate. But long ago, when they'd laid his mother to rest, Charlie's dad had said something Charlie knew he'd never forget.

"People talk about there being a lot of fish in the sea," his dad had said, "but there was only ever one for me. That was your precious Mama. From the moment I laid eyes on her, I was completely undone. That was it," he'd said. "You'll know when you find the one who's meant for you, too, Charlie. You'll know."

Charlie wanted to believe his father was right, but he realized he had his doubts, not so much about the knowing part—that part had already come true. It was the practically impossible feat of getting Kate to notice him, too.

Charlie had no illusions of grandeur. He knew he could never begin to compete with the likes of Eric, or even Dustin in the looks department. He did know his father was right about one thing, though. Whether Kate ever cast a glance his way or not, there would never, ever be another girl for him.

Charlie backed through the swinging doors of *Virtually Mine's* stock room, balancing his precarious pile of presents. He secured the white velvet box on top, under his chin. As hard as it had been to motivate himself, he resolved that he would do Samantha's bidding. He would give Archie's clients a more reasonable amount of service. It would all be worth it, he thought, if it meant one more moment with Kate.

When Charlie rotated toward the office pool, his eyes widened in shock. There was the company's receptionist, Levon Mink, leading Kate into Samantha's office. Charlie teetered back and forth, unsure what to do. A box of candy hearts slid off of his stack and, as he tried to catch it, the whole load went flying.

As hard as Kate tried to keep herself calm, there was something about Samantha Raznick that rattled her right from the start. From the moment Levon introduced her, the woman's steely gaze never left her. Kate waited for Samantha to blink, but it seemed that she never did. Kate could feel Samantha studying her, head to toe, as she waltzed around her desk.

"You look vaguely familiar to me," Samantha murmured.

Kate shifted self-consciously. "I can't imagine why."

Sam strode across the office toward Kate. "Let's get right to it then, shall we, Ms. Mae? You are not, nor have you ever been in any way, shape, or form, associated with the Equal Employment Opportunity Commission."

Kate fought for composure. "I can explain about that."

"No need. I admire your pluck."

Astonished, Kate lowered her defenses a tad. "You do?"

Samantha tipped her head toward the busy office pool outside the glass walls of her office, amused. "And though I take a certain pleasure in surrounding myself with men, perhaps I've been missing out on a substantial portion of the market."

Kate could hardly believe her ears. "I was thinking exactly the same thing."

"No, you weren't," Sam presumed. "You're a starving actress looking for a paycheck in a saturated field. But I suppose your face could do rather well for us in a homespun sort of way."

Kate mulled it over. "Actually, I don't want to be a face."

"You don't."

Kate braved a step toward Samantha. "I want the hands on, nitty gritty. I was thinking I could maybe be an Operator."

Sam arched her brows. "You. A worker bee."

Kate nodded, her confidence growing. "I can stir up the honey."

Once again, Kate could feel Samantha studying her. Exactly what was going on in the woman's head, Kate didn't know, but she could tell from Samantha's tightening gaze that the wheels of consideration were turning.

Finally, Samantha gave Kate an affirming nod. "Yes, Ms. Mae. I'm sure you can."

Were it not for Eric's sudden appearance at the door, Kate might have relaxed. As it was, she quickly turned from him, hoping against hope that he wouldn't notice her.

Samantha motioned Eric toward her. "Eric, come in. I take it you've signed out with business affairs."

Kate reeled as Eric stepped into the room.

Samantha smoothly gestured Eric toward Kate. "Eric, this is Katherine Mae. We're talking about branching into Imaginary Girlfriends."

Eric smiled warmly at Kate. It was hard for Kate to read exactly what he was thinking, but clearly he recognized her. He almost seemed to be enjoying this happenstance.

As Kate reached out to shake Eric's hand, her eyes pled with him not to say anything. It helped that Samantha turned aside and sauntered back toward her desk.

Kate shook Eric's hand a little more briskly than she normally would have, lightly emphasizing her words. "Eric, how nice to meet you for the very first time."

Eric winked at Kate cooperatively. "Yes, my pleasure."

Greatly relieved, Kate turned back to Samantha. "Ms. Raznick, why don't you go ahead and tend to your business with Eric. I can just wander around, you know, get the feel of the place."

Samantha slid open her desk drawer. "You do that, Katherine. See if you can get one of the drones to acquaint you with the basics."

Mouthing her thanks covertly to Eric, Kate backed out of the office and closed the door.

As Kate ventured into the office pool, Eric watched her go, intrigued. There was something about Kate that set her apart from most all of the girls he'd met in L.A. Even in this ruse of a context, there was a certain genuineness in her eyes, something he hadn't seen in anyone else in a very long time.

The fact was, Eric was so distracted by tracking with Kate as she passed through the Operator's cubicles that he didn't notice Sam's return until she cleared her throat just behind him. This time, he would not let Samantha Raznick get the better of him. He turned back, and seeing his final check in her possession, he instinctively reached for it.

With a retaliatory air, Samantha withdrew the check smoothly and tapped it against her arm. "Interesting, the way it went with you Eric. A blaze of glory, then nothing. You do understand that though, sadly, our Operators are favoring other Imaginaries of late, your face will still inspire your pre-existing hits throughout the term of the original license."

Eric rolled his eyes. "Whatever." He reached for the check, half-knowing that she would still make him wait for it. Samantha was becoming predictable to him, and try as she might, he resolved that he would not let himself be drawn in by her again. As arresting a woman as she had seemed to him at first glance, she had lost her power over him. He stood his ground, silently waiting.

A moment or two passed before Samantha put the check into Eric's hand. Her expression hardened. What beauty she had left her face. "Do let me know if you should ever...reconsider."

In a way, Eric felt sorry for Samantha. He stood toe to toe with her, holding her soulless gaze. "No, thanks. I think we're done."

As M.J. trudged up the stairs to her apartment, she hoped she could get inside without seeing any of her neighbors. What with all the mud on her clothes, there would be questions, questions M.J. wasn't exactly in the mood to answer. She was almost home free. At least she thought she was, till she spotted Dustin, sitting outside her door, flossing his well-groomed teeth.

Dustin looked up. "Yikes! You look horrible."

M.J. fumbled for her key. "Thank you, Dustin. Your opinion is oh, so crucial to me. What are you doing here?"

"Waiting for Kate."

Heaving an exasperated sigh, M.J. unlocked the door. "Well, she's not back and I'm not staying. Turns out I suddenly have laundry."

Dustin stood to his feet. "Hey, do you own a dictionary?"

M.J. marveled at just how random Dustin could be. "Kate does. Why?"

Not waiting for an invitation, Dustin waltzed into the apartment. "Reesa says I need to woo Kate. But would she tell me what a woo is? Noooooo. She's all "look it up." Is that even a real word? I mean, woo?"

M.J. followed Dustin in and extended a palm to direct Dustin back to Kate's room. "Who am I to stand in the way of higher education? Middle shelf. Before her journals."

As she watched Dustin go, M.J. found herself pondering what Kate had ever seen in the guy. Sure, he was good looking. He'd been okay for a laugh here and there. But one thing was for sure: he was no Rob Galloway.

Suddenly, M.J.'s eyes brimmed. She did her best to shake it off, but didn't find it easy. It wasn't just that she was alone again, or that Dustin didn't make good company. It wasn't that she'd lost her job writing parking tickets. What it was was that, for once in a very long while, she had allowed her spirit to soar, her heart to hope. Now, she was free-falling, and reality was a long way down.

Wandering through the office pool of *Virtually Mine*, Kate passed station after station, checking their Operator numbers, and smiling at the average Joes who manned them. She paused, interested to watch as Operator 37 drew a heart on each of a stack of homemade cards. "Are those for your clients?"

Operator 37 grinned at her. "I like to give it the personal touch."

Kate nodded. "That's really nice. Hey, would you happen to know where Operator 52 is stationed? He's supposed to train me."

Operator 37 knitted his brow quizzically. "She taking girls, now?"

"Looks like."

Referencing a list, Operator 37 stood to look over the surrounding cubicles. "Operator 52, that's Butters. He was just here." He turned to the next Operator. "Torkinson, where did Charlie go?"

Kate emitted an audible gasp. "Charlie Butters is Operator 52?" As she fought to absorb the shock of it, she noticed Eric, striding toward her from Samantha's office.

Eric pocketed his paycheck. "So, it's Katherine Mae? See, I thought it was Kate Valentine."

"Shhh! It's—yes, it's Kate, but—oh, this is so completely loaded. How'd you know my last name?"

Eric shuffled adorably. "Okay, please don't think I'm a stalker because I swear I'm not, but...I met you and you seemed really nice and so my type, and I sort of checked out your info card at the casting studio. Don't hate me."

Reeling at the turn of events, Kate floundered. "No, it's... I don't know what this is."

Eric cupped Kate's elbow, charmingly leading her aside. "Look, maybe it wasn't an accident that we ran into each other, that they put us together, you know? Maybe there could be something here."

Still struggling a bit to regain her bearings, Kate pondered the notion. "Maybe. I'm... Eric, I'm kind of on cerebral overload at the moment. It's like a multi-car pile-up on the neural highway. So...please, I really hope you don't take this personally, but I've gotta go."

As quickly as her feet would carry her, Kate bolted from the office. She had no idea what she'd say or do when she got where she was going. All she knew was that, no matter what, she desperately had to find Charlie.

Newly educated concerning the meaning of the word *woo*, Dustin slid Kate's unabridged Webster's back into its place on her bookshelf, flanking a full row of her journals. Wooing was all about winning her heart, he realized. But why it was that Kate didn't think he knew her mystified him. What difference did being able to tell her things about herself that she already knew make? Besides that, how was he supposed to find out all that stuff when she was hardly even talking to him anymore?

All of a sudden, Dustin realized that those bits of extraneous information about Kate he needed to know might be right in front of his nose, nestled beside Kate's way-too-thick dictionary, waiting to be discovered in her collection of journals.

"Oh, this is awesome!" Dustin crowed as he pulled the first in a line of Kate's journals out. With a self-satisfied grin, he made himself comfortable, cracked it open, and began to read.

eleven

Wistfully, M.J. loaded her dirty clothes into a washer at the Fluff and Fold. Soon, all the evidence of her disaster of a day would be rinsed down the drain and into laundry history. She supposed she could have waited till her usual washday, but the idea of those grimy togs taunting her from the basket at the bottom of her closet was just too much to take.

When it came to humiliations of this magnitude, M.J. preferred to keep short accounts. The sooner her ill-fated deeds could be put behind her, the sooner she could pick herself up and move on with her life.

So it was, with as much determination as M.J. could muster, she reached for her detergent. It was then that she made a discovery. There, in her otherwise empty laundry basket, was a hand-lettered flyer.

In and of itself, finding a flyer wasn't all that unusual for M.J. People hawking their goods and services left flyers all over the place in Santa Monica. In her day as a Meter Maid, she'd switched out many a flyer for a parking ticket on an all too littered windshield.

Reflexively, M.J. reached into her wash basket to toss the flyer, but its simple headline arrested her attention:

No time to do your laundry?
Call Rob Galloway: Laundry-Doer Extraordinaire!

M.J. looked up from the page, hardly able to believe her eyes. There was Dr. Rob Galloway, standing tall with two boxes of washing powder.

Rob's dimples accented his grin. "So, were you thinking color-safe bleach or active oxygen?"

Her mind whirling, M.J. studied the situation. It couldn't be, but it was. "Wait a minute. Okay. You don't do your clothes here. Do you?"

"Nope. I totally followed you."

A light dawned for M.J. "Then you're here for..." Her eyes widening in disbelief, M.J. tentatively pointed to herself.

Rob shrugged playfully. "I just saw you around, strictly in a laundry-spotting context, and thought this might be a good way to meet you."

M.J. nodded, taking it in. A landslide grin spread across her lips. "I grew on you, didn't I?"

Charlie sat quietly in his apartment, waiting for the other shoe to fall crashing down in front of him. As much as he wished he could persuade himself otherwise, he knew his cover had been completely blown. He'd slipped out of work as soon as he heard Kate chatting up his fellow Operator, the one who had quickly volunteered his name.

Kate would want to talk to him now. She was so sensitive in that way. She would tell him how much she valued his friendship, what a great guy he'd be for someone else, and that would be that.

The time for pouring his secret passion into poems and gifts had passed. Mostly though, what he realized he'd miss were the phone calls, time spent conversing with the girl who had utterly stolen his heart.

The more Charlie thought about it, the more he realized that there wasn't a soul on earth that he could talk to about any of what he was going through , certainly not Mrs. Teasdale, and least of all Kate. He considered phoning his father, and then a wave of shame washed over him for masterminding the charade in the first place.

How could he admit to his dad that he'd done what he'd done when he couldn't even tell him what V.M. Enterprises really was? Charlie thought about how proud his father had been when he landed a computer tech job in the big city. (That much he'd been able to share honestly.) Though it had only been part time, it had been a foot in the door, his dad had encouraged, a building block for better things to come.

There was nothing wrong in an honest day's work, Charlie knew, but as much as he'd rationalized that *Virtually Mine* was just brokering harmless fantasy, he admitted that the spirit of it wasn't entirely harmless, let alone honest. As he sat there, he came to grips with the truth, that behind every Imaginary Boyfriend was a real-live person, who was connecting with another real-live person, stirring up real-live emotion in real-live hearts.

Charlie looked up to the only One he could bear to face when he knew he'd totally blown it. Even that took everything in him. "I knew better, and I still..." A tear slipped down Charlie's cheek. "I let you down, I know. But that isn't the worst of it," he whispered. "I pulled Kate into this, too. And I'm really, really sorry."

"Charlie!" Kate called as she knocked on his door.

There she was. She'd come to clear the air with him, just as he'd known she would. He wiped his face, wondering if she'd heard him.

Again, Kate knocked, this time more insistently. "Charlie, would you please just talk to me?"

Charlie sat, paralyzed, unable to respond.

"Charlie, I know you're in there."

So, she had heard him. Still, nothing in Charlie was ready to face Kate yet. As soon as he faced her, he knew it would be over, something that could wait just a little while longer.

Dustin closed the last of Kate's journals as he overheard Kate's calls to Charlie, coming from just outside.

"Charlie, please!" Kate implored.

As quickly as he could, Dustin fumbled to set each of Kate's journals back in place on her shelf.

"Charlie," he heard Kate continue. "I'm going into my apartment now, but please come and see me, okay?"

Realizing his time was nearly up, Dustin dashed out into Kate's living room. "Prepare to be wooed," he exuded as he sat on her sofa, intent upon looking casual.

As Kate entered, a look of surprise darted across her face. "How did you get in?"

Dustin rose. "M.J. was here." Bursting with excitement, he pointed to Kate's blinking answering machine. "Okay, get ready. That message light, that's Wissy. And your mom called."

Kate knitted her brow. "You listened to my messages?"

"Well, I was here," he explained, "and it was on speakerphone, out loud, but anyway, you booked that commercial Wissy's working on, right off the tape." Kate didn't look anywhere near as excited as Dustin had expected. In fact, she looked completely blasé.

"I did?"

Dustin cocked his head to the side. "Uh, yeah."

Kate grimaced. "Oh, great... My big break with hygiene products."

Clearly unenthused, Kate took off her jacket.

Dustin followed her toward the coat closet. "Kate, this is huge! You're finally in the game. This is what you want."

"I don't know about that anymore."

Nothing in Kate's response computed for Dustin. "What do you mean you don't know?"

Kate hung her jacket and turned back. "Dustin, it's just... I've had this kind of epiphany and—"

"No, no, absolutely not. No epiphanies allowed. Only what's an epiphany?"

Kate finally looked at Dustin. "It's just...all due respect to everybody who does it, but all of a sudden, I don't think I want to spend any more of my life pretending to be somebody else."

"You don't want to be an actor?" Dustin blustered. "What do you mean? Who doesn't want to be an actor?"

"I guess... I guess I don't." Kate stowed the scooter. "I think I want to do something that's more...in my own, actual moment. Maybe teach."

Dustin preened. There it was: his opening to commence with his freshly informed wooing. "Well, you do have your certificate already."

Kate stopped. "Did I tell you that? I didn't think I did."

Dustin couldn't help smiling. This was going way better than he'd hoped. "Hey, I know what your secret obsession is, too."

"You do?"

He leaned in confidentially. "Okay, I don't get why, but it's using grammar good."

Kate shook her head, a bit confused. "It's *well*. But, yes."

Dustin paced, impressed with himself as he rattled on to Kate. "You went to Longhollow College where you majored in Special Ed and had your first stage role as, wait a sec...Tinkerbell, till they dropped your wire too fast and busted your wrist—no, your foot."

Kate's mouth dropped. "How do you know that?"

Dustin nodded proudly. "Oh, I know lots more. You'll be impressed. Okay. You fly in your dreams. Holidays make you homesick. You love Rocky Road, but won't touch Pistachio. You had a life-altering crush on some TV star guy I never heard of, which is partially why you moved out here, hoping to run into him somewhere."

"Who told you this?!" Kate demanded. "M.J.?"

"You doodle in the margins," Dustin continued. "You're double jointed—why didn't you tell me this before? This is highly important data!"

Kate's face went white. "Dustin...what? Have you been reading my journals?!"

Dustin beamed, sure he was scoring major points. "Yeah. I hardly even got bored, either. And I thought it was really cute how you played around with calling yourself by my last name."

Suddenly, the color returned to Kate's cheeks. "Dustin, you don't just... That's private!"

Dustin shrugged, completely confused. "Not from me!"

"Yes, from you! From everybody!"

Dustin pointed a defensive finger at Kate. "But you said you want me to know all your stuff!"

"Not all my stuff!" Kate protested. "Just the parts I want you to know! How am I supposed to even look at you again, knowing you know about—"

"—how you won a ten dollar bet with your Dad by drinking a whole glass of milk through your nose?"

"Nooo!"

Dustin reeled back with laughter. "Dude! Even I think that's gross."

"Auuuuggggh! Dustin, just go home. Go away. Now!"

With more strength than Dustin thought Kate had, she pushed him toward the door. He did his best to resist. "But I'm wooing you!"

"I don't want to be wooed," she insisted. "I want you to get lost, scram, vamoose!"

"No way!" he spouted.

"Every conceivable way!"

Before Dustin could stop her, Kate had shoved him out the door and closed it behind him. Hearing the latch click into place, Dustin yelled through the locked door. "I'm not leaving, you know! I can hold out for hours, maybe days."

Dustin fished into his pocket and pulled out the only thing he found in there. "I've got plenty of floss and I am staying right here!"

Suddenly feeling nature's call, Dustin muttered, kicking himself. "I *knew* I should have used the can."

A roaring fire crackled in the fireplace of Kate and M.J.'s apartment. Kate stood beside it, paging through a journal, just one of many, chronicling the ups and downs, the minutia that made up her days.

Why she'd always felt compelled to write her thoughts down, to record the on-going details of her life, she hadn't known. Given what had happened, though, she was highly motivated to transition to password-protected journaling on her computer. Kate took a last sentimental look at a hard cover journal then added it to the blaze. There were a lot of journals, she realized. This fire would burn for a long time.

M.J. unlocked the door and entered with her fluffed and folded laundry. Kate wasn't sure if it was the firelight or if M.J. was actually glowing.

M.J. put her basket down. "Okay, guess who has a date tonight? A real one."

"Not me," Kate rued. "Not I. Listen to me. I'm losing all sense of syntax."

M.J. motioned outside toward their apartment building's common area. "You do know that Dustin is in the pool?"

Kate rolled her eyes. "You must mean that guy I am never letting near me again."

M.J. grimaced. "Not so much on the wooing?"

Kate resituated her journal with a fire poker. "Not so much."

With Dustin lounging by the pool, Charlie was confident that Kate wouldn't venture outside, not after the spat he'd overheard. So, seeing as he still had his management responsibilities to attend to, he decided it was as good a time as any to do some maintenance on the pool.

At first, Charlie thought his presence might encourage Dustin to leave, but Dustin never budged. He just sat, sprawled on a lounge chair, his pants soaked waist to cuff.

Charlie cleared his throat. "You done in there?"

"Yeah."

Charlie picked up a bucket of chlorine crystals, just as a deliveryman rounded the corner of the building. The guy headed up the stairs with a showy bouquet of flowers.

Dustin sat up. "What's up with that?"

Charlie inched around Dustin's lounge chair, trying to get to the edge of the pool. "Excuse me...uh...just..."

Finally, Dustin scooted aside. "Might want to give it an extra go, there, Bud. Some kid went swimming and I think he might have marked his territory."

Absently stroking her stuffed polar bear, Bubba, Kate slumped on her bed. She half watched as M.J. sorted through her clothes. It wasn't so very often that M.J. had an actual date, much less went out shopping for one, so the pickings in M.J.'s own closet were understandingly slim.

M.J. pulled a cute top out of Kate's things. She held it up against herself, the tag still dangling from the sleeve. "Oooh-la-lah. You sure you don't mind? You haven't even worn this."

Kate set the polar bear aside. "Go ahead. It's not like I've got anyplace to go tonight."

"Don't pout," M.J. replied. "How many billions, correction, zillions of nights have I stayed at home while you went out with Dustin?"

Kate knew M.J. was right. "Sorry. But couldn't you have warned me how hideous it feels?"

"Not adequately." The look on M.J.'s face conveyed that she well recalled what it was like. She wandered over to the bed and took a seat by Kate. "You gonna be okay?"

As she looked at the polar bear beside her, Kate could only sigh. It was what it was, and she'd just have to get through it. She only perked up a little when the doorbell rang. "Probably Charlie."

Kate scooted off the bed and went to answer the door. Talking to Charlie wouldn't be easy, and she still didn't know exactly what to say, just that she needed to say something. On the other hand, if it were Dustin, there was no way she'd let him in, no matter how long he waited.

Kate peered out the peephole. Surprisingly, Kate found it was neither Charlie nor Dustin outside. Instead, she opened the door to a stunning floral arrangement.

The deliveryman smiled congenially. "Kate Valentine?"

Kate glanced at her watch. "Yeah, that's right. Isn't it kind of late for deliveries?"

The deliveryman affirmed it with a nod. "Guy paid me triple. Must be crazy about you."

M.J. wandered out just as Kate brought the arrangement inside, shut the door, and opened the card. "Aloud please."

A bit taken aback, Kate read:

Congrats on booking the commercial. Guess what? I did, too! Let's grab dinner tonight and celebrate. Eric (310) 555-5763

"Who's Eric?" M.J. inquired.

Kate's attention lingered on the card. "Eric is Brad, only really Brad isn't Eric, he's Charlie who's pretending to be Brad, who supposedly looks like Eric."

M.J. waived her arms in confusion. "Wait, wait. Charlie? As in our apartment manager, Charlie?! He's your Imaginary Boyfriend?"

"Not the face," Kate explained. "That's Eric. The real person behind the face is Charlie, who isn't, by the way, speaking to me right now, but... Oh, M.J. What am I going to do?"

Mustering her resolve, Kate marched down the apartment building steps and approached Dustin where he slept by the pool. She cleared her throat. Nothing. She nudged his chair.

Finally, Dustin's eyes popped open. An impish expression quickly unfurled. "I knew you'd come down."

Kate stood her ground. "Dustin, you have to leave."

Dustin sat up. "Okay, maybe I shouldn't have read your journals."

Incredulous, Kate shook her head. "Maybe?"

"Probably," Dustin conceded. "Okay, definitely. But come on, now, Kate. You gotta know I was just trying."

"Trying to what?" Kate blustered. "To mortify me beyond words, to wholly and categorically creep me out?"

By then, Dustin lumbered to his feet. He stood a respectful distance away. "I was... I'm trying to say I'm sorry, that's all. I want you back."

Kate expelled a deep sigh. As clueless as Dustin was, this time, she knew at least his heart was in the right place. Completely embarrassed, she hid her face in her hands. Through the cracks in her fingers, she could see him coming closer, bending down from his taller frame to look at her eye to eye. Playfully, he peeled her fingers away from her cheeks.

Her anger subsiding, Kate still put up resistance. "Cut it out."

"Not till you smile for me," Dustin insisted. "Gimme a little snicker."

Despite Kate's best efforts, she could feel the beginnings of a smile as it curled on the corners of her lips.

Dustin lit up, encouraged. "Ooh, I saw that!"

Deliberately, Kate pouted. "I'm not smiling. That was a twitch. I hear twitches are quirky."

For once, Dustin seemed to get her joke. He shuffled his feet sheepishly on the concrete. "Kate, see, the good news is, I retain very little."

"Who knew that would be such a plus?" Kate quipped.

"Except the nose-drinking part. That's probably going to stick."

Kate shrugged self-effacingly. "Yeah, I figured. With the visual."

Dustin moved even closer. "So..."

Kate put her hands up, stopping him. It felt good to be back on friendly terms, but she knew that friendly was all they would ever be. As cute as he was and as much as she'd tried to convince herself otherwise, he was not the one for her. "Dustin, I... Okay, here it is: I have a date."

Dustin's face fell. "With who?"

twelve

Charlie edged the blinds open to peer outside of his window. He had seen the bouquet arrive earlier. He had seen heard Eric's confident knock on Kate's door and put two and two together. He'd listened to the ease with which Eric greeted her. Now, he watched as Eric took Kate's arm and led her down the stairs to leave. Even Charlie had to admit that they made a sensational looking couple.

It wasn't about conceding defeat for Charlie. Defeat would have meant there was ever some semblance of a competition, and it was plain enough for Charlie to see that if this had been a race, he hadn't even made it to the starting blocks.

Charlie did his best to face up to the facts. As much as he wished it could have been otherwise,

Samantha had been right. Kate was entirely out of his league.

Though he always did his best not to judge, deep down, he'd never thought Dustin had been anywhere near worthy of Kate. However, in fairness, he had to admit that Eric could be an entirely different matter. As pretty as Kate was, she deserved a guy as handsome and personable as Eric appeared to be, a guy who seemed poised for success.

Charlie didn't know exactly why Eric had resigned from *Virtually Mine*, just when he'd rocketed to the top of their stable of Imaginaries. But whatever the reason, something in Charlie respected that Eric had suddenly opted to leave their roster. A year of witnessing the dynamic between his boss and the models that she hired left plenty of room for supposition. Somehow, Charlie had a feeling about Eric's sudden departure. He wanted to believe the best about him, especially if he was going to be seeing Kate.

Quitting *Virtually Mine* on principle was more than Charlie had yet brought himself to do, he realized. Maybe there was some substance beneath that eye-candy face of Eric's. Maybe he was a smart, stand-up guy. Maybe he would treat Kate the way she deserved to be treated. For her sake, Charlie hoped so.

As he watched Kate and Eric disappear down the sidewalk toward the Promenade, Charlie coaxed himself to hope they'd have a good time. They'd go to dinner, maybe a movie, he supposed. They'd trade tales of what brought them to L.A. They'd revel in the amazing way they had met, how it seemed so meant to be. They'd stroll past street musicians, soulfully singing of romance in the city of dreams.

It wasn't long before he heard Rob arrive to pick up M.J. for their date. From the confines of his bachelor apartment, Charlie watched as they headed off toward the beach with a picnic basket.

Though Charlie had never liked being alone, he'd long ago accepted it as his lot. It hadn't ever been easy, but on this particular occasion, it ached like never before.

Kate thanked Eric for a lovely evening out, and then entered her darkened apartment. He had been a true gentleman, she reflected. It was a rarity that she greatly appreciated.

Altogether, it had been quite a day.

As Kate's eyes adjusted to the moonlight, spilling in from the front windows, she stopped, stunned. There, in the middle of the living room, was the Victorian chair she'd sold to Charlie, the one with the scratch on the leg from her childhood ice skates.

When Kate flipped on a lamp, she caught her breath. A white velvet jewelry box rested on the chair's brocade seat. A single fresh daisy had been placed on top.

Moving closer, she found that an envelope was tucked under the box. It was labeled *Open Me Last.*

Kate stood there for the longest kind of time, just looking at all that Charlie had left for her. Reflexively, she welled up with emotion over everything that had transpired. In a way, she was afraid to open either the white velvet box or the envelope underneath. "Oh, Charlie," she murmured. "What did you go and do?"

Finally, Kate picked up the jewelry box and lifted its hinged lid. Tucked inside, with a golden heart necklace, she found the keys to her old ragtop convertible. A scrap of paper attached to the key fob read:

Up and running again.

Overwhelmed, Kate sat down. She stared at the envelope for a while. With a deep breath, she opened it and pulled out the hand-written letter. As she read, she could almost hear Charlie's voice, pouring out his heart:

Dear Kate,

It's been one of those days. I'm not entirely sure why it is that there are so many things I have to say to you, and yet, I cannot manage to speak a word of it to your face.

Perhaps it's my IBS acting up. Perhaps it's just my fears. But certainly, it is because I've been in love with you for so very long, and I can't bear seeing in your eyes that you don't return it.

Kate looked up soberly, her face washed with regret. Mustering her courage, she continued to read:

I'm quitting my job tomorrow. I'll be turning in my notice as apartment manager, too. Maybe I'll move to the valley. Maybe I'll go home for a while. Maybe I'll just get on a bus and see where it takes me.

It'll be easier this way, Katie. You'll go on gracing the presence of every person who has the great blessing of meeting you. And I'll always know that for the sweetest week of my whole unremarkable life, the most beautiful girl in the world was virtually mine.

Kate buckled over with sobs. Rivers ran down her reddened face. She wept harder and longer than she'd ever wept, far more than she'd wept over Dustin. She realized that she had long loved Charlie as a friend, but never once had she considered the possibility that there could be something more.

Tears gave way to prayers, prayers more fervent than she'd prayed in a very long time. "Oh, God," she cried. "What am I supposed to do?"

Late that night, Charlie sat alone in a Ferris Wheel car on the Santa Monica Pier, watching the thinning crowd as they returned to their cars. It was his final night on the Wheel, he had decided, one last look over the shimmering city, one last reminder of his very best memory: watching Kate enjoy this very ride, and seeing the light of her smile.

Though the ride had ended, Charlie sat relishing a few more moments of what he was reluctant to end. In the morning, he would pack up what little he owned and head for a visit home. He would tell his father everything. They'd put their heads together and figure out how he could start anew.

That's when the ride attendant's voice wafted into Charlie's ears. "Closing down. Sorry," the ticket taker said. Charlie didn't turn, not at least until he heard another voice, that voice he'd come to adore.

"Is there any way you could run it one more time?" Kate pleaded. "Just this once?"

Seeing her, Charlie didn't know whether to hope or hyperventilate. As hard as he could, he fought doing either. Instead, he sat paralyzed in wonder as she charmed the attendant into cranking up the ride for one last whirl.

Time stood still. At least, it seemed to as Kate approached and boarded Charlie's car. Though he couldn't bring himself to look at her directly, he could sense the warmth of her smile.

Charlie swallowed hard, knowing he had to say something. "How'd you find me?"

"I know you, Charlie," she replied. "Just like you know me." Kate lowered the safety bar. "How long have you been riding?"

Charlie glanced at his watch. "Couple, three hours."

Kate nodded. "Sounds like a personal best."

A burst of courage came over Charlie's heart. Okay, maybe not a burst, but a nudge more than he'd ever had with Kate before. "I saw you met Eric," Charlie admitted. "He's the one you fell for. I mean, I couldn't be more hetero and even I know he's, you know, very...visible."

Kate nodded thoughtfully. "Yeah, Eric seems like a very nice guy, but to tell the truth—" Kate stopped mid-sentence as the Ferris Wheel began to move. "Ooh. Here we go."

Charlie braved a glance in her direction. "You don't have to—"

"Actually, I do," Kate added. "Some matches, they look good on 8x10 glossies. They do. But...truth is, the whole time I was with Eric, I couldn't help thinking about you. Not just who you were as Brad, but who you've always been to me as you. It's your heart I fell for, Charlie."

Charlie felt his jaw drop. "You. Fell for me."

Kate nodded. "Really did." She shivered in the night air. "Kind of chilly tonight."

Pulling sheepishly at his tee shirt, Charlie finally found words. "I sure wish that I had a jacket to give you."

Amusement danced in Kate's eyes. "This is the part where you put your arm around the girl and offer to keep her warm."

Charlie shook his head. "I, uh... I couldn't."

"Look at me, Charlie."

Charlie mustered his courage. He turned his face toward Kate's. As he did, for the first time, he noticed the golden heart necklace, glittering around her neck.

"Charlie, I don't know where this will go. All I know is...I adore you. And I'd like to give us a try."

Charlie fought for air. "Dry throat. Very dry."

Kate reached out and took Charlie's face in her hands. Sincerity glistened in her eyes. "I like how you look. Your face, it...it just shines with everything that you are." Slowly, she drew him into an exquisite first kiss—gentle, promising, and pure.

As Kate's lips parted his, Charlie gazed at her, dazzled. "Throat's better. Definitely getting better."

Encouraged by her musical laugh, Charlie braved kissing her back, and then, almost as quickly, he broke away. "I'm not, by any chance, imagining this, am I?"

Kate looked deep into Charlie's eyes, deeper than he remembered any girl ever looking at him before.

"No, Charlie," she glowed. "This time, I'm pretty sure it's for real."

about the author

SUSAN ROHRER is an honor graduate of James Madison University where she studied Art and Communications, and thereafter married in her native state of Virginia.

A professional writer, producer, and director specializing in life-affirming entertainment, Rohrer's credits in one or more of these capacities include: a screen adaptation of *God's Trombones;* 100 episodes of drama series *Another Life;* Humanitas Prize finalist & Emmy winner *Never Say Goodbye;* Emmy nominees *Terrible Things My Mother Told Me* and *The Emancipation of Lizzie Stern;* anthology *No Earthly Reason;* NAACP Image Award nominee *Mother's Day;* AWRT Public Service Award winner (for addressing the problem of teen sexual harassment) *Sexual*

Considerations; comedy series *Sweet Valley High;* telefilms *Book of Days* and *Another Pretty Face;* Emmy nominee & Humanitas Prize finalist *If I Die Before I Wake;* as well as Film Advisory Board & Christopher Award winner *About Sarah.*

Among the books she has authored, Rohrer's previous fictional titles, *Merry's Christmas, What Laurel Sees,* and *Bright Christmas: an Amish love story* are also from the REDEEMING ROMANCE series, a collection of inspirational love stories adapted from Rohrer's original screenplays. *The Beautiful World* is Rohrer's novelization of her screenplay, adapted from Eleanor H. Porter's beloved classic book, *Just David.*

REDEEMING ROMANCE

More Redeeming Fiction

Nonfiction by Susan Rohrer

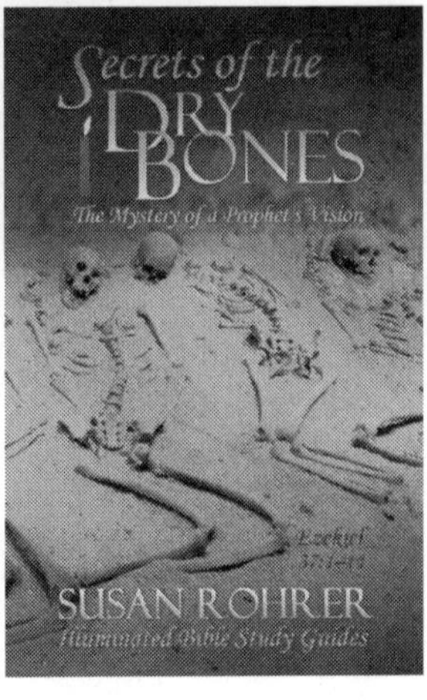

A Final Note Before We Say Goodbye

Dear Reader,

Thanks so much for the time we've spent together as you've read this book. I hope you enjoyed reading it as much as I did writing it.

Would you consider posting a quick review? It's easy. Just go to the review section of this book's page on Amazon. You'll have the opportunity to share your reading experience with family, friends, and other readers across the world, and I'll truly appreciate your feedback.

Gratefully,
Susan Rohrer

Manufactured by Amazon.ca
Bolton, ON

41007227R00118